“I

Antonia's brother indicated Michael with a flourish of his hand.

Antonia glanced at Michael, who was strangely still, and shook her head. “I can't drag Michael into that sort of scheme,” she said.

“The idea does have merit,” Michael quietly observed. “I think we should consider it.”

Bowing her head, Antonia played with the strings of her reticule. The thought of entering a false engagement with Michael was more than she'd reckoned on.

Michael gave her hand a comforting squeeze. “I know I haven't exactly fostered your confidence in the past,” he said softly. “But I promise to do my best to see you come to minimal harm. Can you bring yourself to trust me, Antonia?”

She returned his searching gaze, a multitude of questions buzzing in her head. Finally, after long moments, she spoke. “I haven't any choice but to trust you, Michael.”

With her life, she was sure she could. But with her heart?

THE SCHEME OF THINGS

JANEANE JORDAN

Harlequin Books

TORONTO • NEW YORK • LONDON
AMSTERDAM • PARIS • SYDNEY • HAMBURG
STOCKHOLM • ATHENS • TOKYO • MILAN

Published January 1992

ISBN 0-373-31166-4

THE SCHEME OF THINGS

Printed in U.S.A.

PROLOGUE

EYES NARROWED, MISS Antonia Marley peeked through a tangle of branches and leaves. Her intent gaze scanned the myriad hues of summer's offerings, and her ears strained for the slightest sound.

On the wings of the playful breeze rippling the clear waters of the millpond came the soft thud of hooves. She tensed, fingers closing over the nostrils of her horse, lest the dainty black mare whicker and expose their presence. A sigh escaped before her lips curved into a cat-in-the-cream smile.

Maddening, provocative man, she mused. The mere sight of Lord Michael Alton, the Earl of Montewilde, set her heart tripping. He sat his huge black with a careless, graceful confidence, his tanned hands resting lightly on the reins.

How she loved him! Every fibre of his lean, athletic form, every dark hair waving in the thick short-cropped mass about his head... She admired the way he wore his white linen shirt, half unbuttoned, exposing the strong column of his tanned throat; the way his buckskin breeches moulded so perfectly to his muscular thighs.

He disappeared behind a line of trees. Her grip on the mare's nostrils loosened, and she stroked a hand down the velvety muzzle. Securing the reins, Antonia sank onto a fallen log.

"I know I shouldn't do this, Fancy, darling," she murmured to the dainty black, lifting a foot to divest herself of one half-boot. "But my lord Alton returns to London two days hence, and I must receive a declaration before he goes. I've heard of women cunning enough to entrap a man into marriage, and there simply *has* to be an agreement between us before he enters that den of scheming females! I can't bear to lose him—my heart would surely break were he to wed another!"

Her shoulders sagged; a mournful sigh escaped her lips. She tugged at the second half-boot, dropping it beside its mate. "So how otherwise am I to bring him to his senses, Fancy, girl?" she queried. "He still considers me the child he knew before leaving for Oxford five years ago! Does he imagine I stayed in pigtails whilst he gained his three-and-twenty years? I'm seventeen, certainly of an age to be wed!" She tossed her head. "I vow I'd make him a perfect countess!

"He isn't indifferent to me, Fancy, dear," she continued in a rallying tone, her fingers deftly working the buttons of her riding habit. "I sense it when he looks at me in his considering way. He's ever so friendly... but so frustratingly playful. Vexing man! He treats me like I was twelve! 'Sissy-britches Annie'—oh!"

As she stood, the habit fell to her feet. She surveyed her slender—and yes, womanly—form, clad now in a thin chemise. A saucy smile curved her lips and a martial gleam entered her eyes. Contemplating the silent mare contentedly munching the lush summer grass, Antonia gave a half shrug.

"Well, Fancy, love, today his oversight shall be rectified. Michael won't be able to ignore I'm now quite grown. And, what's more, he'll realize he loves me, and will declare his intentions of marrying me!" Her smile softened. "Oh, how I'd love to be his wife!"

She ruffled the mare's mane. "He'll be riding homeward soon. I must go. Be a good girl and warn me if anyone else approaches."

Stepping from the limp folds of her riding habit, she slung it over the branch of a nearby tree and turned to the mill-pond. Carefully scrutinizing the surrounding area, she drew a deep breath and left her hiding place.

The water's icy shock soon dissipated. She plunged into its cool depths. The smooth surface gracefully gave way to ripples as she glided back and forth, her gaze sharp on the line of trees where Michael would reappear. Her heart pounded harder, but her resolve never wavered.

She swam for what seemed an eternity, worrying now that after all her careful planning, he'd fail to show. Her strength waned, her breath became laboured, but her vigil was finally rewarded. In an instant, she put her plan into action.

With a strangled, yet audible gasp, she bent double, submerging herself. After a few convincing struggles, she surfaced. Uttering a feeble squeak—and gulping a hasty breath of air—she sank and struggled more. She wasn't required to surface again. Strong arms closed about her, dragging her upward.

"Don't fight, Annie, don't be afraid. You're safe—I've got you."

Michael's words soothed, though a trace of fear underlined his tone. Sputtering and coughing for effect, Antonia threw her arms about his neck, clinging tightly. Her shoulders shook against his masculine chest.

Michael swam to the shallows and carried her to shore. She rested her head on his shoulder, content to play the invalid. Her clinging wet garments couldn't fail to alert him she was now a woman.

He held her closely, his chin buried in the wet strands of her hair. She thought she detected a feathery kiss before he lowered her to the grassy turf.

"'Sdeath, Antonia! What a fright you gave me! Are you all right?"

She nodded, still gasping for breath.

"I can scarce credit I was so close to help! What happened, did you get the cramp?" He brushed a wet tendril off her cheek, his voice rich with concern.

"I think so," Antonia groaned, pressing her hand into that area of her anatomy where she imagined a cramp would form. His gaze left her face, sliding down her slender frame. She knew a wonderful satisfaction at his sudden sharp intake of breath. Stretching as if to relieve the pain of constricted muscles, she thrust her breasts upward and arranged her legs more seductively on the soft turf.

Any fears that he'd find her unattractive were immediately laid to rest. His breathing quickened and smouldering passion darkened his eyes to onyx. He seemed mesmerized by the rise and fall of her heaving chest, by the gentle curves of her flat midriff, and he inhaled deeply.

"Michael?" She drank in his face, tousled hair, thick lashes, his sensual mouth promising the kiss she'd desired since his return to Montewilde Park ten weeks ago. She trailed her hand down the wet shirt clinging to his muscled arm and he caught his breath. Sinking down beside her, he gazed at her from heavily lidded eyes, seeming to fight an inward battle. Then his lips claimed hers in a kiss which swept away the world and left her drowning in a delicious morass of burgeoning desire.

His tongue traced her lips. Hers parted, opening like a flower to the sun. She drank deeply, savouring every moment of abandonment, every touch of his thumb gently caressing her neck, her face, her ear.

A soft moan escaped him. One hand pressed the small of her back, the other sampled the dips and curves of her figure. Antonia surrendered to the heady excitement of power, the delightful sensation of newfound passion.

His questing hand slipped beneath her chemise, making startling contact with a chilled breast. Reality intruded. She uttered a surprised squeak. Pushing his hand away, she stared accusingly into his passion-drugged eyes.

"What is it?" he asked thickly, gathering her close and trailing kisses down her slender white throat.

"What *is* it?" she repeated indignantly, ineffectively trying to manoeuvre his lips farther from her cleavage. Panic threaded through her veins. This wasn't going according to plan...she hadn't dreamed he'd take such liberties! "You were supposed to declare yourself, not ravage me!"

He dragged his lips from a precariously close encounter with one partially exposed breast. *"What?"*

The enormity of her error stunned her. Stricken, Antonia stared at him in mute, agonized helplessness. Her lashes fluttered down, and she gave a tiny cough, modestly adjusting the straps of her chemise. When her lashes lifted, Michael's eyes had narrowed to hard, glinting slits. A strangled oath escaped him. He pushed away, slamming a clenched fist onto the grass.

"Declare myself?" His face loomed closer, a sneer twisting his lips. "I'd expected better from you, Antonia. Egad! When Hamsley's daughter sneaked into my chamber, I scarce believed her audacity, but came to understand her desperation. I quit that scene on the instant, hieing myself home to escape the clutches of scheming, lying females. And now you." His tone, dangerously low and controlled, matched the fire in his eyes. "By the heavens, Annie, if you're pregnant, too, I'll strangle you."

Antonia scooted away, pressing a shaking hand to her chest. "How dare you?"

"How dare *I?*" he queried with tight-lipped anger. "You devious little baggage! A cramp, indeed!"

He leaned towards her. She scrambled to her feet and backed away, blinking against the sting of tears.

"No theatricals, I beg," he lashed out. "Surely you have more cards up your scheming little sleeve than this. Do you tell your father you've been dishonoured by the Earl of Montewilde? Or do you hope to shame me into offering for your hand? Which is it, Antonia?" An agile movement brought him to his feet. He loomed over her. "Where did you get it?"

"Get what?" she croaked.

"Your bag of tricks. You seem well-versed in the art of seduction." Her mouth gaped with shock, and his lips curled in derision. "Why cry halt? Wouldn't it better suit your purpose to be thoroughly and undeniably compromised? Or did you think I might know better than to carry through, and thus, you were waiting for a ring?"

Every awful word pierced her heart. She backed away, mesmerized by the anger and disappointment in his dark eyes. He mustn't know how much she loved him, or how badly he'd hurt her. "You're a beast, Michael," she quavered. "A horrible, wretched beast. And you're wrong."

She brushed away a tear and stomped to the tree where she'd so carelessly flung her habit.

"Was I wrong in believing you planned this . . . this rescue?" he stormed, dogging her heels. "Listen to me, m'girl, you've *not* been compromised by *me*. I have nothing to fear, because I'm going straight to your father to tell him he'd best keep a very close eye on you."

Her fingers, fumbling with the buttons of her habit, stilled. She blanched and whirled round. "What?"

His lips curled again. "Don't worry. My story will be brief. You were swimming nearly naked in the millpond, where you got a cramp and I chanced to save you."

"Why say anything?" she cried. "I shan't say a word!"

He laughed sarcastically. "I put no stock in your word, Antonia. I've had enough of swooning females calling compromise, all agitated nerves and affronted sensibilities. I shan't reenact such a scene with you."

He stood inches from her, and before she thought twice, she slapped his cheek hard. "You rat!" she spat. She refused to betray the fright she experienced at the sight of his set and angry features as he fingered the reddened skin. "Do your worst, Michael. I've nothing to hide. I assure you nothing, absolutely *nothing* would force me to marry you. I would as lief die."

By riding Fancy hard, she had nearly reached home before Michael caught her. She had hoped he'd grant her grace, but he strode up the steps beside her, requesting an immediate interview with her father. Grasping her wrist, he propelled her into the library, where they were joined by Lord Marley. Michael explained the mishap, concluding, "I kissed her, sir, but in no way dishonoured her. I leave you to judge what next action is best."

Antonia sat in fulminating silence. That all her carefully wrought plans should end so disastrously was frustrating, but the knowledge that Michael didn't love her—indeed, now hated her—was unbearable. Her hands clenched as her father pronounced judgement.

"You're an honourable man, Michael. I see no reason to make more of the matter." He eyed the lingering marks on Michael's cheek. "Unless you feel otherwise, Antonia?"

For one vicious, spiteful second, Antonia considered making Michael realize his worst fears. She'd know satisfaction in pushing him over the brink, in some small way making him pay for the hurtful words he'd flung at her. She gazed into his cold, expressionless eyes. "No, sir. I beg you'll not force me to marry him, for I should hate it above all things."

"Very well, that's an end to it," Lord Marley proclaimed. "Michael, I can't thank you sufficiently for rescuing my daughter. May I pay for your boots?"

"Certainly not, sir. And you're very welcome. I bid you good day. Miss Marley." He gave her a perfunctory bow and left the room, his wet, ruined Hessians squishing with every step.

CHAPTER ONE

THE GLOOM IN THE SHABBY private parlour of the King's Castle—quite a pretentious name considering what the inn had to offer—was only partly dispelled by the small fire sizzling on the hearth. Rain pattered softly against the window, intensifying the heavy atmosphere. A chilly draft seeped through the inferior window-sashes, making the room's few candles sputter at regular intervals.

Lord Michael Alton, Earl of Montewilde, shivered, though he scarce noticed the flickering candles or the drizzle. He had eyes only for the grey-haired gentleman clad in the sober attire of a solicitor.

That man shifted uncomfortably. He glanced towards the third party and shrugged with finality. "Those are the terms, gentlemen. Not to be prosaic, but—" his brows lifted expressively "—to the victor belong the spoils."

"Well!" expostulated the second young man, breaking a stunned silence. "I've never heard a more daft, hare-brained and *addlepated* scheme in my entire life!"

Alex Harvey, a tall, coldly handsome individual, had sandy hair which glinted with threads of gold. His eyes, a curious mixture of green and grey, resembled a murky sea. Straight nose and high cheekbones attested to his aristocratic superiority, and Michael knew he could command the ladies with a quirk of his sensitive lips.

A black scowl now marred his fine features. Michael watched silently as Alex tipped his chair, crossing one elegantly clad leg over the other. "The old man had windmills in his cockloft. The whole notion is demmed absurd."

The solicitor cleared his throat. "Mr. Harvey, the terms are quite valid. The will was duly witnessed and signed. Having had ample experience with this type of affair, I made sure George McAlver possessed the entirety of his wits." A note of defence for his own, wholly respectable character underlined each clearly stressed word.

"As I explained, your great-uncle George was greatly burdened by the loss of those lands. Since the death of his wife, he had imbibed too frequently too often which made him quite careless at games of chance. His card partner didn't know the circumstances driving him, any more than he knew that McAlver's great pride would forbid him to re-purchase the acres. 'Twas all fair and square, but had your uncle been sober, he'd never have staked that particular section. He was flooded with guilt and remorse at its loss. He didn't rest easy until he'd hit upon this scheme."

A belligerent scowl darkened Alex Harvey's face. The solicitor sighed audibly and, straightening his papers, returned them to a leather-bound case. "Even had your uncle humbled himself to repurchase the acres, 'twould have been of no use. The lands were immediately entailed in the dowry of the aforementioned young lady. Poetic justice, McAlver thought. Those rich lands had come to him through his own bride's dowry; 'twas fitting they return to his heir through a bride's dowry."

He snapped the leather case shut. "It's incumbent upon one of you—" he glanced at Michael, then Alex "—to marry the girl, and restore the acres to the estate. The estate and the fortune will give you the needed incentive to see all is done accordingly." His brows drew together. "Shall I re-read the will, Mr. Harvey?"

Michael's lips quirked in a half grin.

"That won't be necessary," Alex growled.

"Very well. You're both shrewd enough to realize allowing the young lady any suspicions for your. . . er, courtship, would be folly, indeed. McAlver was quite serious, and I'm sure neither of you would see his money endowed to a farm for indigent animals.

"The ton will know of McAlver's passing. Should questions arise about your expectations, answer that the will's validity is being questioned. Rumour has it McAlver may have written and hidden another. That should buy you the time needed to woo and win your bride."

He pulled on black gloves. "Two other rules. Marriage over the anvil at Gretna Green won't be tolerated, and you're not to defame each other's character. A triumph by either method, and the other receives the inheritance. Be assured, gentlemen—" his pale blue glance encompassed both men "—my eyes will be open."

He lifted his hat and walking stick. "I trust I've explained everything satisfactorily? When the matter is settled, we will meet again. You have my card should you have any questions."

Gathering his case, he nodded and crossed to the door, extracting a serviceable handkerchief from his pocket. Applying it to his flushed face, he muttered, "Thank God that damnable business is done!"

A funereal silence reigned for some minutes after the door closed. Finally Alex shuffled, and demanded harshly of his silent companion, "What think you of this queer start, m'lord?"

Michael soberly surveyed the other man. Scarcely six months his senior, Alex was as unlike him in looks as in character, as fair as Michael was dark. In contrast to Alex's sleekness of style, Michael preferred an easy, laughing manner.

The laughter, however, was absent now. He shrugged a shoulder and inclined his head, refusing to vent his wealth of frustration. "May the best man win."

"I can scarce credit this calm acceptance of your fate, Montewilde," Alex scoffed. "It's more than a bout of fisticuffs we're about to engage in. 'Tis a *fortune,* man! I don't care what that solicitor said, McAlver had bats in his belfry. What if she'd already been wed?"

"Since she isn't, we needn't consider that aspect."

Alex's lips curled and his narrowed eyes glinted. "You haven't a prayer, Montewilde, if you plan to best me. It hasn't escaped my attention that she turns you the cold shoulder. Methinks there's a reason why, but—" he waved a slender hand dismissively "—I shouldn't care to be bored with it. My advice, however, is that you begin a search for an heiress."

"If you're so certain of victory, Harvey, why are you snivelling like some demmed invertebrate?" Michael retorted.

"Because I don't relish taking on an expensive female to obtain what's rightfully mine! A blasted nuisance and nothing else."

"You forget I'm as entitled to the money as you," Michael quietly reminded him.

"That's just it. Why couldn't the old codger divide the blunt between us and have done? The estate doesn't *need* those acres—the sentimental fool! He was rackety, make no doubt." Alex stood and pulled on his gloves, adjusting them with short, angry movements.

"Well, I'm off. Say au revoir to the fortune, Montewilde. By fair means or foul, I'll win it." He sketched a polite bow, incongruous with his nasty words, and left.

Michael frowned into the silence of the room. There was no love lost between him and Alex. Though they were often labelled cousins, no blood ties existed between them. Both preferred to consider the other merely as a "family connexion." Alex Harvey was related to George McAlver through George's wife, while Michael was the grandson of George's sister.

He brooded into the dying fire. What evil genius had prompted Uncle George to pit one nephew against the other? He'd certainly cooked up an infamous scheme, which didn't bode well for the pawns in the game. One of them would be deeply disappointed, and he didn't want it to be him. He'd set great store by the inheritance from Uncle George and desperately needed it. He hadn't waited like a vulture for the old man to stick his spoon in the wall; however, it had been pleasant to dwell on what his half of the octogenarian's immense fortune could do for his straitened circumstances.

Sighing, he dropped his head to his hands. Yesterday had seen Uncle George laid to rest. With a passing sadness for the inevitability of death, Michael had yet offered silent thanks that the death hadn't been for nought. His uncle's legacy would change the lives of his heirs, and also Michael's tenants, farmers, and all who depended on him for their bread.

Today for the first time in years Michael had felt lighthearted, unburdened of the gross responsibility of managing an estate and providing for countless lives on an uncomfortably limited budget. He had ideas which, when implemented, could employ many men, and he eagerly awaited moving into action. His bubble had been mercilessly burst.

Michael groaned. What a time for the old duffer to get such a maggoty notion! And what a bride to choose! Harvey had correctly assumed Michael's chances for meeting her at the altar were slim. She scarce paid him the time of day. He snorted. How could he have guessed that day three years ago that he was casting away his future security? Damnation! The odds were assuredly against him, and Harvey had such cursed good luck with the ladies.

Pouring another glass of wine, he swallowed it, taking no notice of its inferior quality. He tapped his finger against the glass, pondering how to make his peace with the damsel, but no scheme came to mind. She was unmovable in her stance towards him, though he'd tried to apologize several times.

Drat it all! Harvey would waste the wealth in his gaming hells. His once-plentiful coffers already showed the strain of his loose living. He spent freely, sparing no expense on baubles for a mistress or on another fancy piece of horseflesh. Knowing he had Uncle George's money behind him allowed him to continue his hedonistic lifestyle.

Michael shuddered at the idea of Harvey winning the bride. The man was a dashed cold fish. He'd make her miserable. Not that Michael bore any feelings of love for her, but after all, their families were friends and he'd practically grown up with her. They'd been on good terms, too, until she'd pulled her madcap trick. Indeed, he'd been quite taken with the Beauty his sissy-britches had grown into, and he had considered her a prospective bride.

He closed his eyes, remembering her loveliness, her softness, her desirability. His anger, his accusations, his slur on her innocence. He'd wanted her desperately, and was mad as fire at himself for nearly taking her despite her protests. Enraged that she'd set out to compromise him, he'd almost thrown caution to the winds and let her. He grimaced. If they overcame that obstacle, 'twas possible they could rub on tolerably well. . . . *If* they overcame that obstacle.

His frown deepened. He poured another glass of watered wine, considering and rejecting several ideas. Two facts, however, remained of paramount importance: he needed the money, and he made no doubt that Alex Harvey would make a poor husband. Somehow, he had to impress the latter upon her—or upon someone who might influence her.

He drained his glass, pondering the wisdom of such a move. Deciding he'd nothing more to lose, he tugged on his gloves, picked up his hat and made his way out of the inn and into the drizzle.

Three hours later, he greeted his pleasantly surprised host. "I'm in a devil of a coil, sir," he confessed. "I thought it wise to beg your assistance."

CHAPTER TWO

THE COACH AND FOUR swept up the long drive, swung wide and came to an abrupt halt, nearly tossing its occupant to her knees. She barely managed to save herself by grasping the worn leather strap. Dignity affronted, she frowned with displeasure at the driver's lack of consideration, and righted herself with as much grace as possible. She thought to give him a setdown, but decided it wasn't worth it. Retrieving her reticule and bonnet from the dusty floorboards, she swatted at both and placed the bonnet back on her head.

Drumming impatient fingers on her reticule, she finally realized he wasn't going to help her down. Biting back her brother's favourite curse, she opened the door and stepped out. Her frown vanished at the sight of her imposing, if slightly dilapidated, home. At last! She'd thought she would never arrive. The trip from London had seemed interminable. No stops for a refreshing cup of tea, and indeed, only one for a quick change of horses. That old bear of a driver hadn't cared one jot for her comfort.

At least, she noticed grudgingly, he'd managed to secure a footman for her scanty, hastily packed luggage. Pausing a moment to school her features, she drew some coins from her reticule and handed them over.

The driver counted slowly and silently, then gave a slight cough. "Eh, lookee 'ere, miss, this 'ere—" he indicated the coins in his grubby palm with a slight nod "—ain't wot we agreed on."

Biting her lower lip in an effort to contain her frayed temper, she stared hard at the burly, shifty-eyed man. Without a word, she stretched forth her hand. He cocked his head, shrugged and dropped the coins into her open palm.

Slowly, and in clipped tones, she counted them aloud, returning each with a deliberateness that would've warned those who knew her better not to press her further. When the last coin fell into his thick palm, she folded her arms. "So you see, my man, that *is* the amount we agreed upon."

"Eh, and so it is," he conceded without hesitation. "Tol' me missus jes' t'other day, ain't good wit me numbers, I ain't. Was sure you was a couple pence short." He produced a small, battered purse from the pocket of his dusty coat and poured the coins in with much rattling and jingling. "Thankee, miss." He exposed yellow teeth in a grin which was almost a leer, returned his purse to its resting place and sauntered away.

She shuddered. How could she have allowed that unsavoury character to drive her all the way from London? "Good riddance," she muttered, and coughed as a cloud of dust from the departing coach enveloped her.

Turning on her heel, she gained the wide stairs. At the door, Fellow's dubious glance slid from the retreating coach to her. He looked pointedly behind her, as if expecting another body to miraculously materialize.

"Good afternoon, Fellows," she greeted him, removing her bonnet and gloves. "As you can see, I'm quite alone."

"Miss Antonia," the butler acknowledged, not betraying disapproval by so much as a flicker of an eyelash. "We weren't expecting you. Shall I have your, er, luggage taken to your chamber?" He eyed the untidily packed portmanteau with disfavour.

"Please." She laid her bonnet, gloves, and reticule on the occasional table adorning the spacious hallway. "And where might I find my brother?"

"In the blue salon, Miss Antonia. If I might say so, I don't believe he's in any condition to receive the peal I perceive you're about to ring over his head."

"Well, ready or no, the disreputable rascal is going to hear it," she said with an appreciative chuckle. She squared her shoulders and marched off.

The door to the blue salon was open. She paused on the threshold to observe the indolent creature ensconced in a stuffed chair. One leg draped lazily over an arm of the chair, one hand held a glass of brandy. The decanter reposed within easy reach.

"It must be difficult to refill your glass, brother dear," she observed in her driest tone.

"Why, Antonia, my own dear sister," Rodney drawled, not bothering to look up. His slurred speech attested to the fact that he'd been nursing the brandy for some time. "And it's not difficult at all, you see. I just place the glass on the table, pick up the decanter, and voila!" He suited his actions to his words, topping up the glass and sloshing liquid over the sides.

"How clever," was her vinegary response.

"Anyway, thought you were in London."

"I was. I just arrived." More than a trifle put out to find her brother inebriated, she decided to launch the attack none the less, even if he weren't quite coherent. "So," she began sternly, "perhaps you might explain just what you've done, Rodney Marley."

Rodney cocked his handsome head to one side. "Not very observant, sister. Anyone can see I've addled my drink with strong wits." He hiccuped to confirm the statement.

"At this precise moment, I'm interested in neither wits nor drink," she snapped, "but in the consequences of your ill-considered actions regarding Maria." All the frustration she'd stifled during the long ride from London poured forth in a passionate diatribe. "In the event that you've obliterated it from your mind, I would remind you that you were engaged to nearly the wealthiest, and quite the prettiest, heiress in all of England. For some unknown reason—one beyond my comprehension—she chose you above all her other suitors. And you jilted her!"

Unconcerned, Rodney took another gulp of brandy. Antonia stared at him incredulously. "Have your wits gone a-begging? Look at this place! It's falling to ruin. It used to hold a position of pride in the county, but now...look at this chair!" She jabbed a merciless finger into a sizeable hole. "The upholstery needs replacing!"

She stalked to the windows. "The curtains are tattered—their pattern has faded quite beyond recognition." Flicking back a dusty drape, she gazed at the yard. "The roof needs work, the lawns want clipping and the gardens are a shambles. We've had to dismiss half the servants, and this table has collected an inch of dust!

"In case it's slipped your mind—" she wagged an accusing finger "—this place will belong to you one day, and Papa's not so flush in the pockets anymore. What are you going to do in five years? Go abroad to escape your creditors?" Breathless at last, she struggled for control. "I'd like an explanation."

"Couldn't abide the chit. Too much like you." Her brother took another gulp from the nearly empty glass.

"Couldn't abide her?" Antonia exclaimed in disbelief. "Hah! She was your only saving grace! And you're going to make yourself ill if you don't quit slurping that devil's brew as if it were water."

Rodney ignored the sisterly advice. "Who told you, anyway?"

"Not the person who should have," was her huffy answer. "I saw Maria in Bond Street and thought to have a word with her. She gave me the cut direct. How humiliating! You can't imagine all who saw. Your ears should be burning, for surely all the tabbies in Town have their heads together over this affair. I'd like to have died of mortification! I managed to get a word with her abigail. Her abigail!" she added scathingly. "Not my brother."

"Oh, take a damper," he exclaimed, then chuckled perversely. "Sure would've liked to see that setdown, though."

"Rodney! What a perfectly beastly thing to say. You should've received the setdown, not I. The only reason I got the cut is because I've the misfortune of being your sister."

"Misfortune, is it?" Rodney bristled. "I'll have you know it was this face—" he thrust forward that part of his anatomy and flicked a curly black lock from his forehead, "—these deep blue eyes and this—" he ran a finger over his hairy upper lip "—sophisticated moustache which appealed to Maria."

"I'm happy to hear it wasn't your personality," she countered drily, "lest I should suppose Maria singularly lacking in taste."

"And my manly figure," he mumbled defiantly.

"You conceited popinjay!"

"You couldn't understand why Maria accepted me. Only enlightening you."

"So now enlighten me as to what you intend to do."

He waved an unconcerned hand. "Oh, as to that, well... all is not lost." He looked into his empty glass, frowned, placed it on the table and refilled it.

Antonia shook her head at his clumsy attempts. "You've another heiress up your sleeve, I suppose?"

"No..." he replied slowly. "But I imagine my sister should fetch a good bride-price. Heard m'father talking about it just last night. Lord Wilson, you know. Been ogling you this past age." He delivered this blow with all the concern his indolent figure suggested.

"Oh, no. No, No, No!" Antonia shouted, stamping her foot. "I will not! He's as old as Papa, his teeth are yellow, and he's fat and bald. His two daughters are the haughtiest old harridans I've ever seen, and I won't marry him! You're not getting out of this so easily—do you hear me, Rodney Marley?"

"The whole house can hear you, m'dear," a deep voice boomed. "Really, you could at least have shut the door," Lord Marley admonished, stepping into the room and closing it decisively behind him. "And Rodney, perhaps it'd be best if, in future, you leave such sensitive subjects to those who can impart them with some tact."

Antonia flew to her father and clutched his sleeve, her blue eyes lifted imploringly to his. "Papa, tell me this isn't true!"

Lord Marley removed the hand crushing his starched sleeve and patted it. "I'm sorry, m'dear," he said, casting her a commiserating glance, "but something has to be done."

Antonia gazed at him with mounting alarm. "You would sacrifice your only daughter to that ugly old fop? Your grandchildren would have monstrous big noses and bulging eyes!"

If she expected to win her parent over by this argument, she was mistaken. "I have a big nose, m'dear," was his dry rejoinder.

"Well... but not so overly huge, Papa, and your eyes don't bulge."

"Lord Wilson's eyes only bulge when he looks at you, Antonia," Rodney contributed.

"I'll have none of that taproom talk in my salon, Rodney," his father rebuked. He waited for his son's mumbled apology before turning to Antonia. "Speaking of bulging eyes, miss, mine nearly did when I saw that . . . that conveyance which brought you here. Are you lost to all propriety? It's bad enough your brother is, but I expect a little refinement from my daughter. That coach was the roughest equipage I've seen in many a day, and the driver was no more genteel."

"He was quite surly," Antonia admitted reluctantly. "You saw him?"

"From my chamber window," he confirmed, to her dismay. "I need not say you wouldn't have been the brunt of his rudeness had you come attended. 'Tis not the thing for young ladies to cavort about the countryside unaccompanied, as well you know. Now, why didn't you come chaperoned, and in your aunt's carriage?"

Her father had always deplored her impulsiveness; upon reflection, Antonia admitted she'd been rather rash. "Well, you see," she began, choosing her words carefully, "I had to give Polly, my maid, the day off so she could tend her mother, who is ill. I then discovered the milliner had done a faulty job with my new bonnet, so I summoned a footman to walk with me to Bond Street, since Aunt Mattie was taking luncheon with Mrs. Hadley and couldn't accompany me. I needed the bonnet repaired by Friday for the picnic I'm to attend that day—"

"Antonia. I don't need a step-by-step account of your every move. I'd merely like to know why you're here."

Smiling weakly, she drew a deep breath and launched into a hasty but colourful description of her encounter with Maria. "I could scarce credit it, Papa," she finished with a wounded look. "I was quite bowled over and rushed home with the intention of leaving immediately. You must see I had to confront Rodney!"

The implacable expression on her father's face assured her he certainly didn't.

"I couldn't very well take the carriage, since Aunt Mattie had it," she rushed on. "And I knew if I didn't start soon, 'twould be necessary to travel after dark, and that Aunt Mattie wouldn't countenance, so I'd be forced to wait another day. I simply couldn't wait, so I hired a hackney to take me to the nearest hostelry. Thus, the boorish driver."

She sighed contritely. "I admit I wasn't thinking properly. But you might be pleased to know I did have enough wits to leave a note for Aunt Mattie." Her voice ended on a meek and hopeful note, but after one peek at her father's scowl, she grimaced.

"So now I'm put to the inconvenience of sending a much-needed footman to inform her of your safe arrival."

Antonia shrank inwardly. "I'm sorry, Papa, truly. But I was so distressed, and thought it quite the shabbiest trick for Rodney to leave me to find it out in such a way!"

Lord Marley sighed and shook his head. "I can see my children have sorely missed the teaching of their mother. I'd hoped, Antonia, that sending you to your aunt would've curbed some of your hoydenish actions, but I see my hope was misplaced."

"Oh, but it wasn't, Papa!" she cried, rushing to her aunt's defence. "Aunt Mattie has done superbly. She's taught me all the graces—what a lady should and shouldn't do. 'Tis only under extreme duress that I forget. I assure you, she'll be mortified over this. I'll return straight away tomorrow and spare you the need of sending a footman."

"One has already been dispatched," was his dry response. "I've sent a note to your aunt, instructing her to inform whomever it may concern that you are indisposed. There will be enough scandal attached to our name from what Rodney has done; we certainly don't need your behaviour aired about to add to it.

"And you shan't be leaving here until the day after tomorrow. Rodney will accompany you, as I've no intention of allowing him to sulk in the country. I'll send round and invite Lord Wilson to dine with us on the morrow. I'd have you look your best and behave your prettiest."

Antonia, eyes narrowed with uncertainty, searched his face for any tell-tale sign of teasing. It wasn't like him to come the heavy hand. His face was set and inscrutable, however. With a sinking heart, she realized he was indeed resolute. Her mouth tightened stubbornly. "Has he made an offer yet?"

"As yet, he has no idea I'm considering him a prospective son-in-law. My intentions will be made known to him soon enough, and I daresay two hints shan't be necessary before he follows the direction I'm leading."

Her father's voice sounded crafty, as if he were gleefully contemplating the weaving of his monstrous web. For one wild second Antonia thought he'd surely run mad.

"You're playing with me!" she cried. "Papa! *Lord Wilson?* You'd sell your own daughter? This must be a hum! You can't seriously expect me to repair your fortunes by marrying that odious man!"

Her father bristled. "I can expect you to do what I command!" he snapped. His clipped tone warned her not to push. "May I remind you that you've yet to reach your majority, and until that time, or until you marry, I'm your keeper. Your actions assure me you need a firm hand, and I shall hasten to see you get one."

Irresolute, Antonia stared at him. This was surely the worst day of her life. Tears gathered in her eyes and she blinked rapidly. It was imperative she not lose her composure; she must make a final plea.

"Surely there's another way?" she cajoled.

"None that I can see. Rodney succeeded in cutting off all hope in that direction, so I've really no other choice." He frowned thoughtfully. "There may be one small alternative. The Season has nearly six weeks before closing, and you're already financed. There's no reason not to finish it. If you receive a suitable offer from a gentleman whose fortune matches Lord Wilson's, *and* who is willing to pay a handsome settlement, I'll reject the offer I'm sure to hear from our neighbour. Understand I'll not forgo my plans for dinner tomorrow, nor my intention of bringing him up to scratch. I'll merely contrive to keep him dangling until the end of the Season."

"But Papa, that's a near impossible task! In light of what Rodney's done, I'll be fortunate to attract any suitor, much less a rich one. No man wants a penniless wife, especially one whose name is besmirched. I shall be avoided like the plague!"

"I hope we can trust to your aunt's good name to keep you in high standing with Society, Antonia. You've had offers before, and you were penniless then, too. But if you do fail, well..." He shrugged.

Antonia directed a malicious glare at her brother, who snored drunkenly, his glass tipped precariously in his slackened grip. She could've strangled him with no compunction whatsoever. Her gaze returned to her father and she lifted her head. "If I fail," she declared dramatically, "well then... then I shall just kill myself."

CHAPTER THREE

ANTONIA EXHAUSTED the remainder of the evening by pacing through her sitting-room and bedchamber, muttering aloud as she alternately lamented her predicament and mentally abused her father, her brother, Lord Wilson and poverty. She refused to present herself at dinner. When a tray was sent up, she confiscated the pot of tea and returned the rest untouched. Not until she slipped into bed after all was dark and quiet did her brain begin to propose possible solutions on how she might extricate herself from this situation.

The next morning found her tired, decidedly more composed, not one whit closer to an answer, but determined to find one. She entered the breakfast parlour at mid-morning. In spite of the Town hours, she wasn't surprised to find her father lingering over a cup of coffee, reading the morning post. Rodney, obviously feeling the effects of the considerable amount of brandy he'd consumed, was slumped over a plate of barely touched eggs and kippers.

Not by the batting of an eye did Antonia betray her glee at the opportunity presented to extract a small portion of revenge. She bustled brightly into the room and clapped her brother soundly on the back.

"Good morning, Rodney!" she sang merrily and altogether too loudly.

Rodney sank lower in his chair. "Antonia, I'll slay you," he muttered.

Lord Marley didn't glance up from the missive he perused. "Rodney, I'll not have that kind of talk at the breakfast table, if you please. Good morning, Antonia."

"Good morning, Papa," she returned nicely, her polite tone conveying none of her lingering reproach. She crossed the room to the wide double windows and tugged back the heavy curtains. Glorious sunlight flooded the room, and Rodney groaned. Antonia rubbed her hands together in satisfaction.

"Much better, don't you agree, Papa? We shouldn't want you to harm your eyes by reading in the gloom." Smiling sweetly, she made her way to the sideboard and the selection of food laid out there.

"I daresay," was Lord Marley's dry response. His wary glance rested on her serene countenance for a fleeting instant, then he returned to his letter.

Antonia heaped her plate, humming a jaunty tune. Pouring a cup of coffee, she turned to the table, sitting directly beside Rodney. Lord Marley put his letter aside, sighed aloud, and picked up another sealed envelope.

Antonia ate with relish. She savoured a bite of scrambled eggs and murmured, "Such delicious eggs today, don't you agree, Rodney?" But his eyes were closed, his chin sunk onto his chest. With a malicious smile, she laid a hand on his shoulder. "Why, Rodney!"

She was rewarded by his startled jerk. Ignoring his baleful glance, she chattered on. "I don't believe you heard a word I said. I was commenting on how delicious are the eggs this morning, but I see you haven't touched yours. That's really too bad of you; Cook gets most upset when dishes are returned untouched. I told you that devil's brew would make you ill, but there's nothing like good, cold egg to reverse the condition."

She reached over to his plate, speared a bit of egg with his fork, and dangled it under his nose, smiling wickedly.

Rodney, with an expression of distaste, pushed the fork away. "Antonia, will you stop?" he growled. "Quit pestering me." He turned to his father, his expression changing to one of entreaty. "Sir, get this madwoman away from me!"

Before her father could answer, Antonia chimed in. "But Rodney, since you've finished your breakfast, and I haven't, it is you who should leave."

Rodney pushed back his chair with a screech. "Right. Then I'm off. Sir," he addressed his father, "I shall be riding."

"The very thing!" his sister exclaimed. She smiled widely and rose to her feet. "I believe I'll accompany you."

Rodney groaned. "Father!" he appealed in exasperation.

For answer, Lord Marley grasped the bell pull, giving it a vigorous tug. Obviously he was in no mind to lock horns with her. Antonia knew he was fully aware that she would badger Rodney until her grievances were fully aired.

When Fellows appeared, he rasped, "See that a groom is directed to ride with these two—and mind they don't kill one another! Get!" he ordered his progeny.

"Yes, Papa," an unabashed Antonia murmured meekly. She followed Rodney to the door. "Now see what you've done," she hissed. "We have to ride attended!"

"Antonia," came her brother's surly rejoinder, "when I'm feeling more the thing, I think I'll strangle you."

"Oh, pooh!" she laughed and ran upstairs to change.

The horses were waiting when Antonia reached the stables. Rodney placed his foot in the stirrup and she hurried forward. He wasn't going to escape her. The attendant groom helped her mount, then swung onto his own horse to follow closely behind.

Rodney's black scowl from breakfast hadn't lifted; even so, he surprised Antonia by turning on the groom. "Confound it, Harry," he snapped. "There's no need to follow so close. I'm hardly in fit shape to kill this little baggage, much as I'd like to. Now get back!"

The affronted young groom pulled up immediately. Antonia turned in the saddle, sending him a placating smile. "Just because you're feeling poorly," she rounded on her brother, "you've no right to be a boor! I think that was uncalled for."

"Oh, you do?" he snarled. "Well, and I'll tell you to your head, I've had more than enough from you, too!"

"Oh, you have?" she shot back sarcastically. "Be angry with me if you like, Rodney Marley, but if we're counting up grievances, I've more cause to be at odds with you. It wasn't me who threw over London's richest heiress—nor is it me who needs her money so desperately. It's not my house and lands falling to ruin, yet I'm the one who'll pay for them. Is that fair? Is it fair that I marry that . . . that *odious* man, so you might have a secure future? Well, it's not fair. He's the last man on earth I want to marry!" Her voice broke, and she brushed at a tear with an impatient hand.

Rodney peered at her keenly, his expression one of remorse. "I understand, Antonia," he said with a heavy sigh. "But if I said I was sorry, would it help anything? I vow, I'd no notion our father was so deep in the suds."

"I'm more fearful he's lost his reasoning."

Rodney dismissed her statement with a shake of his head. "No, but I'm sure he's desperate if he'd go so far as to consider Lord Wilson a prospective husband for you. Everyone in the county knows he wants a wife only to give him the son and heir he doesn't have, and I told Father so m'self when I heard him discussing the match with Michael the other night."

"What? He was discussing this . . . this monstrous affair with Michael? Lord Alton? I can scarce credit it! What did he say?"

Rodney frowned in concentration, looking a trifle shamefaced. "Didn't quite catch the whole of the conversation. Rather deep in my cups, you know." He snorted with derision. "Been drinking all the way from London. Heard them talking about some land or something . . . think Michael's near to coming into his expectations, what with McAlver turning up his toes." He shook his head, as if to clear it. "Maybe 'twas that, or something about a will getting lost, or its validity being questioned. . . . Anyway, told 'em I'd broken it off with Maria. Funny thing is, I can't recollect m'father being furious. Expected a reg'lar dressing down, you know."

He grimaced sheepishly, then shrugged. "I must've fallen asleep. Next I heard, Father was mentioning a match between you and Lord Wilson. That's when I told him Lord Wilson only wanted an heir and would be a poor choice if one were desirous of his daughter knowing connubial bliss. Guess they didn't listen. They helped me to bed. Don't even remember my head hitting the pillow."

Head bent, fingers agitatedly playing with the reins, Antonia digested the information. "How could Papa be so indiscreet?" she wondered plaintively. "He's inviting Lord Wilson to dine with us this very evening, intending to toss out the hint that I can be bargained for. I should think he'd be so ashamed he wouldn't tell a soul of his nefarious plans."

"But Antonia, Michael's very nearly part of our family . . . been our friend forever, you know."

Antonia lifted her head, her gaze skimming past the trees to where the waters of the millpond glimmered in the sun. She squashed her sudden wistfulness and set her jaw. "He's not been my friend for some time, and I cannot like the idea of Papa discussing with him how I'm to be sold!"

Rodney winced. "Must you look on it that way? Wilson's rich as Croesus! You could have anything you want."

"He's as old as Papa."

"Another benefit. By the time you're thirty, he'll have given up the ghost. You'll be a rich widow and still young enough to enjoy the fruits of your labours. Er...um, well, you know what I mean," he finished hastily, catching sight of her appalled expression.

"That's ten years, Rodney! Ten years of unmitigated purgatory!" Her mind conjured horrible visions of what she'd have to endure, and she shuddered. "No, the price is too high. And he might very well be contrary enough to not pop off until he's seventy."

Rodney sighed. "You're right. That would be far too much to bear. There must be another way."

Antonia sniffed. "Well, as to that, Papa's magnanimously given me an alternative. I can escape the clutches of Lord Wilson if, before the Season is out, I can catch a husband as rich as he. A swimming task, to be sure! You break off with an heiress, and what does the world see next? Me, casting out lures to well-lined pockets!"

Rodney's features scrunched into a fierce scowl. "May as well let the whole ton see we're a fortune-hunting family."

Her brows lifted at his bitter tone. Money again, if she didn't mistake the matter, and not some paltry excuse that he couldn't abide the chit. Rodney and Maria had seemed like a couple very much in love, and although he wasn't averse to Maria's money, Antonia knew there was no less likely fortune-hunter than Rodney. She would've liked to press for details, but the forbidding frown marring her brother's face cautioned her against probing.

"London's about as thick with wealthy bachelors as it is with fog on a clear day. I thought for hours last night and couldn't hit upon a single man who possesses the fortune Papa craves and the qualities I desire. It's no use, Rodney. I refuse to marry a man I can't abide, and I should certainly hate to kill myself to escape a repulsive situation. The more I think on it, the fewer options I see."

Her eyes narrowed thoughtfully, and she captured her bottom lip between her teeth.

Rodney studied her through red-rimmed eyes, then massaged his temples tiredly. "And those are?"

"First, I'll need your promise to help me in any way you can."

His brows rose in suspicion and he eyed her speculatively. Then his face cleared with dawning enlightenment and he shook his head disapprovingly. "Hold up there, Sis. If you're thinking of eloping with that nodcock Smythe, don't even suppose I'll lend you countenance. The man hasn't a feather to fly with, and he's a profligate as well."

"Hmm, now there's an alternative I hadn't considered," she mused, a teasing twinkle in her eye.

Rodney groaned. "Antonia, you're annoying me. Divulge your scheme and be done with it."

"Your promise first," she demanded.

"How can I promise when I don't know what addlepated notion you have in your head?" came his sour rejoinder.

"I assure you, my notions aren't addlepated." She sniffed. "After all you've done to create this mess, the least I should be able to expect is your promise to help me out of it."

A guilty sigh parted Rodney's lips. "All right, I promise... to anything that's sensible."

Antonia accepted with a nod. "I could elope—that's always a possibility, provided I could find a partner who's agreeable and not totally without means, for I'm sure I wouldn't care to live a life of total penury. We'll have to save every farthing over the course of the next weeks, and if worse comes to worse, I could run away. Perhaps then Papa would repent of his callous treatment. I daresay you should come with me in that event, for it's conceivable he'd then make you offer for Humphrey's dumpling of a daughter. Her dowry is rather rich, I hear.

"The only other idea which comes to mind is to place myself in a compromising position. I'm sure even Lord Wilson would balk at accepting soiled goods."

Rodney's mouth dropped open, and he sputtered in blatant disbelief.

"I am a desperate woman, Rodney!"

"You are a brainless twit!" he blurted. "Not one of those plans carries an ounce of credibility, and the last is by far the most witless thing I've heard you utter. It gives me cause to think 'tis you who've lost your reasoning."

"*I* have lost my reasoning? *I* didn't throw away eight thousand pounds a year!" He bestowed a thunderous scowl upon her, and she repented immediately. "I'm sorry, I shan't mention the matter again. But surely, Rodney, you must see I've few other choices."

"Yes, I do see, but the schemes you've outlined thus far are insupportable. I must have your promise you won't indulge in any of them. There has to be another way."

"What way?"

"How should I know?" he demanded testily. "My head pains so I can scarce think. Give me time to recuperate, and I promise, we'll find a way to get you out of this muddle."

Antonia studied him with thoughtful eyes, wholly unconvinced. She shrugged. "Very well then, but you'd best be recuperated by this evening. I shall have desperate need of an ally, I am sure."

CHAPTER FOUR

SATISFIED, ANTONIA GAZED at her reflection in the mirror. Her long-sleeved gown was pale apricot, its simple design enhanced by blond lace at the modest neckline. A thin dusting of pale powder masked her inconveniently healthy complexion; rouge of a coral hue contoured her high cheekbones. A shiny gloss in the same shade coloured her small, shapely mouth. Her thick black locks were arranged in a sophisticated chignon which was wonderfully severe. Only an ivory comb alleviated its stark simplicity.

She had achieved her goal. The colours clashed with her cool skin tones, making her appear pallid and altogether unhealthy. The neatness with which she'd prepared herself, however, would convince her father she'd done her best. With a smug little smile and a final pat to her coiffure, she turned from the mirror and exited her chamber.

Outside the drawing-room doors she paused, marshalling her resources. She hadn't realized how anxious she would be now that the moment had come. There really was no need to get in a pother about it—she was quite firmly decided that nothing would induce her to marry the man! Expelling her pent-up breath, she lifted her chin and swept into the room.

A few areas in the house were kept up for appearance's sake; the drawing-room was one. The best pieces of furniture adorned the cozy, spotlessly clean interior—an interior now marred, in her eyes, by the unwieldy Lord Wilson, ensconced in her favourite chair. He was the personification of a dandy. A tight, kelly green coat—the donning of which must have given his valet great struggle—matched a green-and-gold-striped waistcoat which barely held in check his bulging middle. Gold-coloured inexpressibles stretched at the seams, and clocked stockings covered his fat calves. A brown wig perched precariously atop his head, its curls artfully arranged to frame his florid face. A large emerald graced his starched white cravat; smaller gems gleamed from the cuffs of his coat. Shiny green pumps completed the ensemble.

Antonia, her bottom lip caught between her teeth, solemnly watched Lord Wilson, with much exertion, heave himself from his chair. Her father set aside his drink and stood also, his raking glance encompassing her from head to foot. She hadn't time to guess whether he approved, for he stepped forward, taking her arm to renew her acquaintance with their guest.

"My lord," she acknowledged, curtsying slightly.

His lips turned up in a condescending smile. "Miss Antonia. A delight and a pleasure to see you again. You've matured since last we met. Was just telling your sire he'd best set about finding a husband for you; ain't no sense in a pretty wench like you endin' up her days sittin' on a shelf."

"I daresay I'm not beyond my last prayers yet," Antonia replied with sugary politeness, and suffered him to take her hand in his pudgy one. It called for more composure, though, to keep from flinching when he placed his wet lips on the back of it. A moment later her father placed a glass in her hand, enabling her to turn away from the bulging eyes roaming her figure all too freely. Surreptitiously, she wiped the back of her hand against her gown.

Settling onto a straight-backed chair, she lifted the glass to her lips. Her gaze flickered over the room. "Where's

Rodney?'' she asked casually, a trifle piqued at his absence and, therefore, lack of support.

''Out eyeing Michael's new bloods,'' came her father's mild reply. ''Michael will be dining with us also.''

She checked the glass at her lips. Over the rim, her gaze caught her father's.

''I see,'' she said tonelessly. In truth, she did not. Her father's game became harder to decipher by the minute. If his aim was Lord Wilson, why include Michael? Why, indeed, expose him to this shameless plot? She swirled the sherry in her glass, pondering the dilemma.

Was he casting Michael her way as a subtle means of escape? She quickly discarded that notion. He was well aware of the breach standing between them. Besides, Michael was a mere pauper compared to Lord Wilson. No, it was easier to believe her father was trying to rush Lord Wilson's hand.

Her mouth turned down at the corners. Using Michael, of all people, as competition against Lord Wilson was a shabby trick. The desire to thwart her father's carefully wrought scheme became more pronounced. Somehow, someway, she would find a means of escape.

The men's conversation slowly penetrated her dark thoughts. Her attention focused on her father's words, ''...a sorry plight, indeed.'' Lord Marley considered his neighbour morosely and lifted one shoulder in a shrug. Lord Wilson nodded in understanding, an avaricious gleam entering his eyes. Antonia's mouth tightened.

Rodney and Michael chose that auspicious moment to join them. Her father greeted the pair, and poured drinks.

''What think you of Michael's new bloods, Rodney?'' Lord Marley asked.

''Beauties—bang up to the mark!'' Rodney enthused. He accepted a drink, turning to give Lord Wilson a courteous greeting.

Antonia had eyes only for Michael, who made his way directly towards her. After three years of knowing polite, and sometimes not so polite, formality between them, she was surprised when he executed a gallant bow. Lifting her hand, he brushed his lips softly against her inner wrist.

"Good evening, Antonia," he said, his husky voice low.

"My lord," she acknowledged with forced calm. She was fully aware his kiss had been most seductive, and that he still held her hand captive. Seldom in the last years had he addressed her by her given name, and then only by a slip of the tongue. Not so this time. Their eyes locked, and in his steady gaze she detected cool control and even the hint of a challenge. She regarded him warily.

Michael's gaze broke contact to assess Antonia. Same little Sissy-britches Annie—never one to take anything lying down. She'd fight to the end, then do precisely as she chose. He'd have to be at his constant best if he hoped to bring her round. He gave an appreciative chuckle. "You did well. You look, er. . . stunning."

"Charming of you to say so."

He quirked a roguish grin, his eyes dancing.

Antonia snatched her hand from his and turned up her nose. She refused to acknowledge his awareness that she'd done her best to look her worst. It irked her that he knew her reasons for doing so. Her father handed him a drink and bid him be seated.

Antonia watched him covertly, noting the trim lines of his figure even as she puzzled over his conduct. He lifted an enquiring brow her direction. She hastily transferred her gaze, only to discover every eye in the room upon her. Rodney regarded her with a considering smile on his lips, her father with a slight frown. Lord Wilson wore an expression of thoughtful calculation. When Fellows announced dinner, Antonia wasn't a little relieved.

Lord Wilson appeared at her side, the arm he thrust out nearly catching her in the shoulder. A quick side-step saved her from bodily harm, and she accepted his proffered arm. He trotted her off towards the dining-room, patting her hand with a nerve-racking consistency. She was settled onto her chair with more haste than grace. When his heel snagged in the hem of her gown, she managed a polite smile.

"Don't mind it," she murmured, shaking her head. His clumsy efforts to disentangle his shoe gave her gown further distress. 'Twas the last shred of proof she needed to convince her that death would be preferable to marriage with this buffoon.

Although the numbers were uneven, Antonia knew no insecurity. She was used to being the only female at table in her father's house. As hostess, a title she gladly would have relinquished, her place was at the foot, while her father sat at the head. Rodney chose the seat beside him, next to Michael, who sat at Antonia's left. Lord Wilson seemed to take up the whole side of the table to her right.

Small talk prevailed through the first two courses, topics ranging from crops to the wily fox which had evaded the local hounds for nigh onto two years. Antonia, content to listen, spent her time pushing the food round her plate. She was ever conscious of Michael's proximity, and humiliated by it. The man she'd have once gladly surrendered to watched with covert, yet avid interest, as Lord Wilson attempted a clumsy flirtation, casting her such amorous glances as to make her blush.

The arrival of the third course provided a slight reprieve. Lord Wilson was inordinately interested in any new delicacy which tempted his palate. The footman departed, and Antonia found her father's gaze upon her.

"Are you feeling well, Antonia?"

Though he seemed genuinely concerned, she knew a waspish satisfaction. It would serve him well if his daughter did become ill at his repulsive plans for her future. All eyes shifted to her once again. Piqued at being the centre of attention, she was, none the less, not dissuaded from her course. She waved a nonchalant hand. "'Tis but a slight indisposition. Nothing to worry over, I assure you."

The answer seemed to satisfy Lord Marley. Rodney diverted his attention, asking, "Are things arranged for our return to London on the morrow?"

Antonia resumed her picking until Lord Wilson, short seconds later, leaned forward to address her. "Do you often get ill, Miss Marley? I declare, you are looking a trifle peaked. Still lovely, of course, but yes, a trifle peaked."

Antonia, containing her jubilation, sighed forlornly and pushed away her food. "Oh, yes," she answered in a soft tone which would in no wise attract her father's attention. "I always get these indispositions. I'm quite, quite sickly."

Michael emitted a strangled sound and began to cough.

Oh, botheration! He would be attending! She directed him a look which commanded his cooperation. "Lord Alton is, of course, familiar with my poor health." She sighed dramatically. "How many times it hindered me from joining him and Rodney at play when we were children!"

"Oh, I do not disbelieve you!" Lord Wilson hastily assured her, though his gaze silently questioned the younger man.

Antonia waited with bated breath. Would Michael be contrary enough to contradict her? Although his expression was sober, she detected the light of mirth dancing in his eyes. Moments that seemed like aeons passed before he nodded.

"Alas, yes," he said. "'Twas always so."

She didn't permit herself even a slight sigh of relief.

"Sorry news, indeed," said Lord Wilson. "I'd always thought you quite, er... robust."

"Not so," she returned on a commiserating note. "'Tis exceedingly tiresome, always having a malady of some sort, but I do contrive, m'lord."

He reached over and patted her hand. "I'm sure you do, m'dear, and very bravely, too. Perhaps though, when you marry, your husband will be able to afford a good physician, and will have the sense to fatten you up a bit. I've found food a panacea for any number of health problems."

Deflated, Antonia found she had no ready reply. His belief in food was quite obvious, but he'd overcome the only weapon with which she had to fight.

"Such a shame though, to spoil so trim a figure, don't you think?" asked Michael, championing her cause.

Lord Wilson waved a thick hand. "Nonsense! Skinny wenches aren't at all to my taste. Got to fatten 'em up, m'boy. Otherwise, you've less than an armful, and there ain't no pleasure to be had in that, no pleasure 'tall."

Antonia's face burned.

She left the men to their port, but scarce ten minutes later they joined her in the drawing-room. She had resumed her seat on the straight-backed chair, shunning the small sofa for fear Lord Wilson would sit beside her. The seating arrangements needn't have concerned her; her father asked her to play and sing for their entertainment. Parading her talents before an unlikely beau hadn't numbered among her plans. More than a trifle indignant, she nevertheless accepted with grace. She lifted the cover from the pianoforte and sat, her back ramrod stiff. Never having enjoyed being the centre of attention, she looked favourably upon Michael as he settled himself on the bench beside her.

"I shall turn the pages and help you sing," he stated matter-of-factly. His quick grin sent her heart fluttering. She smiled her gratification and allowed him to choose the song.

Their voices blended well, his throaty baritone in perfect harmony with her clear lilting soprano. She hit a note, his voice went down and hers climbed higher, and they broke off laughing at the discordant sound which resulted.

"You're supposed to go up there!" she gurgled, nudging him with her elbow.

He chuckled, capturing her arm. The warmth of his hand penetrated her thin sleeve, and she caught her breath. "No, see this little figure here? It means you go down."

She raised her arm, glad for the excuse to break contact. Even his lightest touch engendered the most breathless sensations. "But see this note before it?" She pointed to the page. "It means you go up *before* you go down."

Michael acquiesced to her superior knowledge with an enlightened "Ah," and they began again. This time, a certain amount of credibility accompanied their performance. Their audience applauded, and Michael chose another song. Antonia recognized it as one they used to sing years ago when the confining winter forced the three young people to seek entertainment indoors. Her fingers floated over the first few bars. Rodney exclaimed in delight and moved to join them.

The years fell away, and they entered into the spirit of the song. Once again they were the best of comrades, singing riotously at the top of their voices, making no effort at harmony and sparing no thought for their listeners' ears. The last chords were pounded in tune with their lighthearted laughter.

"Another!" Rodney proclaimed at once, selecting a long-standing favourite. Milords Marley and Wilson groaned in unison. The young people chuckled at their protests and raised their voices in a lively, if somewhat ribald, ditty. Michael's fingers moved to the keys to pound his assigned piece—the only score he'd set himself to learn. His performance was quite rusty, for his hands bumped repeatedly against Antonia's, his fingers covering the keys where hers were playing. She brushed them aside, but not before her timing was destroyed, and they collapsed in laughter.

"Enough," she pronounced, regaining her composure.

Michael rose and extended his hand, bowing from the waist. "'Twas vastly entertaining, fair lady," he murmured.

His actions and words were reminiscent of times past. Antonia placed her hand in his; their gazes locked as he drew her from the bench. A probing question and something less definable spoke from his eyes, holding her captive for long moments. With a sharp pang of regret for the severed bonds of friendship, she turned away.

CHAPTER FIVE

THEY WERE TO DEPART for London in the early afternoon. The dispatched footman brought a note from Aunt Matilda assuring them all was in control. "But," she had written, "for heaven's sake, don't let Antonia be seen entering my house!" So, like a common criminal, Antonia would be bundled back to London under the cover of darkness.

Shortly before their departure, she received a summons from her father. She'd hoped to escape without a final confrontation with her parent, and entered his study with reluctance. He sat at his desk, flipping through some papers, a quill in his hand.

"Ah, Antonia. Close the door and make yourself comfortable."

She perched primly on the chair beside his desk.

His glance flickered over her face. Straightening his papers, he handed her a sealed missive. "Please see that your aunt receives this." He hesitated whilst she placed the letter inside her reticule, then drew a deep breath. "Lord Wilson has made his offer, and it's no mean sum he's willing to settle on you. He assures me he's being quite generous, considering the amount of blunt he'll have to part with to fatten you up, and for physicians." A frown clouded his brow. "Physicians, Antonia?"

Antonia fiddled with the strings of her reticule. "Rodney said he wants a son," she answered in a small voice. "Perhaps 'twas that he referred to."

Lord Marley inclined his head. "Possibly, but he should realize that's one of the responsibilities of marriage. At any rate, I've made good my word. He'll not receive his answer until the Season is over. However, he's decided to remove to London so he might lay claim to you."

Antonia lifted dismayed eyes to his face. He shrugged. "I'm afraid he might put a rub in your way, but there's nothing we can do about it. Michael will accompany you to London, so I rest easy that you'll be adequately chaperoned." He folded his hands together and considered her with keen eyes. "You two were speaking last evening?"

"Yes, I suppose we were," she replied non-committally, her fingers stilling on the reticule strings.

"You're on better terms, then?"

"I'm sure I shouldn't go that far," she returned, sneaking him a wary glance. She recalled the events of the previous evening. 'Twas the first time in three years Michael had exerted a concentrated effort to make amends, and she'd found herself warming to him.

"He hasn't come into his expectations, you know. There's some question as to the validity of his uncle's will."

"What's that to say to anything?"

"Nothing. Just wanted to point out he'll likely be quite wealthy some day, but that he isn't yet."

"So...? If you're warning me away from him, I assure you, there's no need. If you're offering me a way to escape Lord Wilson through him, I must tell you frankly, it's quite impossible."

"Why so?"

She sighed. "You must know, Papa, that we've scarce spoken since... that day."

"Surely it's time to set aside your differences? Forgive and forget? I shan't dictate to you on that score, but Antonia, three years is an extremely long time to hold a grudge."

Mayhap, she thought, again pleating the reticule strings. But what other defence did she have?

ANTONIA'S BROODING GAZE followed Michael through the small square of her window. He was hatless, and his unbuttoned white shirt exposed his tanned throat. She bit her bottom lip. Why must he be so very handsome? So manly? So virile? Why must his buckskin breeches mould so perfectly to his muscular thighs, and his shirt contrast so effectively against his dark skin?

And why, oh why, had she been such a reckless, impatient, foolhardy miss at seventeen? Like as not, had she acted a young lady, he would have given her credit for being one. After the few years of Town bronze she'd acquired, 'twas possible she might even have attracted his attention in the usual way of Society. Ah, what a child she'd been!

She watched as he rode beside Rodney, gesticulating as he talked. Three years later, and he hadn't been caught in parson's mousetrap. Not for want of eager misses, either, nor for lack of matchmaking mamas. While seeming to be indifferent, she had noted the number of lovely young debutantes paraded before his eyes. It wasn't surprising he was considered a prime catch: he was young, handsome and titled, with a fine estate and a grand town house. That alone recommended him to many mamas, but the knowledge that he also had expectations did much to promote him in their eyes.

Antonia gave a delicate sniff. At seventeen, she hadn't cared a fig for his financial position! All that had mattered was her love. Funny how three years could alter one's circumstances. Now a wealthy parti was of prime importance. What made her uneasy, though, was that when she'd searched long into the night for a suitable gentleman, it was

Michael's face which had haunted her—no matter how hard she'd tried to push the vision away.

The fact gave her considerable discontent. Three years ago, she'd vowed never to love him again, never to give him an opportunity to pierce her guard. She shuddered still to think of the destruction wrought that day. Not only had Michael been more furious than she thought him capable, her father too, had been in high dudgeon.

No sooner had the door closed behind Michael than Lord Marley had delivered the severest dressing down she'd ever endured. He was mortified, horrified, scandalized, appalled. He thought her sadly lacking in principle—indeed, a regular hoyden—and graphically described the unsavoury things which could befall a young girl swimming alone in her undergarments. Drowning was the least of them.

She'd listened to his tirade with tears in her eyes, wanting to strike back at Michael by telling the whole, but knowing she'd only lower herself further in her father's esteem. He'd announced she would go to her aunt to learn how a young lady behaved, then he had sent her to her room. She'd locked herself in for days, opening the door only to offerings of food.

Her despair was great, but her anger against Michael was greater still. He'd not only rejected her, but his tattling had added insult to injury. She had vented her spleen by throwing breakable objects at the hearth and cursing him with her pitifully small vocabulary of curses.

Then shame and mortification set in and she'd winced at the thought of her brazen actions. Knowing she'd disappointed her father hurt almost as much as did Michael's curt rejection. She vowed to act more decorously in future.

She arrived in London a willing pupil. Under her aunt's tutelage, she learned how to dress, dance and flirt, as well as behave. By the time she saw Michael again, she was able to face him with a cool dignity. Her aunt, she knew, was informed of their conflict, but with true diplomacy, had never once remarked on it.

Antonia steered clear of Lord Alton, as she chose to address him, as much as possible. To his credit, he'd made several attempts to apologize, but she'd rebuffed his every endeavour. Still, she was forced to speak with him on occasion. Good manners, her aunt maintained, were only good in the face of adversity. Thus Antonia acknowledged him with a chilly politeness.

Until last evening. Somehow Michael had seemed different, almost as if he were determined to override her prejudices against him. He'd made every effort to defer to her wishes. Or was it she who was different? Had her pride received a devastating blow at the mere possibility of marriage to Lord Wilson? At the thought of humbling herself to bring another man, any man, up to scratch?

She sighed, studying her nails with disinterest. Her father was undoubtedly correct—three years was an extremely long time to hold a grudge. However, it wasn't just a grudge. Her behaviour was her defence against Michael. His rejection had hurt so dreadfully, she'd shielded herself by adopting a façade of chilly disdain. It was time, she decided, to drop that mask. Now that her emotions weren't so raw, it would be as easy to be friendly as cold. Besides, only a fool would allow her heart to be broken twice.

The coach rumbled into an inn yard. Antonia saw the familiar sign of the Baying Hound rocking in the light breeze. Ah, dinner! The return journey was proving to be the antithesis of her precipitate flight into the country. Rodney arrived to open the door and hand her down. She gave him a warm smile.

"Go on in with Michael, Annie. I have to see what I can find in a change of horses before I join you." He paused for a moment in silent contemplation. "I told him everything—thought you wouldn't mind."

"He surely knew most everything, anyway," she answered with a careless shrug.

"Not your feelings on the matter. Eloping, compromise..."

She clucked with annoyance. "Rodney, you didn't?"

"I did," he said with a solemn nod. "He's genuinely concerned, and for what it's worth, he's agreed there must be a more perfect solution."

"I am eager for more suggestions, brother dear," she assured him in dry tones. Lifting her skirts, she made her way across the courtyard to join Michael. He was instructing the ostler on the care of his horse, but when she reached his side, he tossed the boy a coin and together they walked into the cool, dimly lit interior of the inn.

The common room was nearly deserted, and Antonia knew a certain amount of relief. The less they were recognized, the greater their chances of thwarting scandal. The innkeeper wiped his hands on a towel and bustled over, asking them their pleasure. Michael bespoke a parlour for three, and he led them to a cozy room. Dinner and a bottle of wine were ordered, the latter of which, along with three glasses, appeared in a trice. Dinner, their host promised, would arrive presently. He bowed out of the room, closing the door behind him.

Silence followed. Antonia, feeling awkward, wandered to the casement to peer out over the quiet courtyard. She suddenly realized this was the first time they had been alone together since *that* day. The thought was unnerving.

"I trust the journey hasn't brought on another of your indispositions, Miss Marley?" Michael asked from behind her.

She turned, to find him pouring the wine. The twinkle in his eyes belied the concern of his words. She laughed lightly. "A slight bout of boredom is all." Her gaze flicked over him in a contemplative study. "Thank you for coming to my rescue last evening. Papa would've been furious had I been caught out in a lie." He proffered a glass of wine, and she moved to accept it. "Why did you do it?"

He sampled his own glass, then lifted a careless shoulder. "I saw a lady in distress, and came to her rescue."

"I'm surprised you didn't tattle afterwards." The words were out before she could stop them.

His brows snapped together, and he looked more than a trifle disconcerted. Then he laughed. "Well done, Antonia! A capital hit, I assure you."

He crossed to the stone hearth, above which reposed two swords. He took up one, tossing the other in her direction. Instantly recalling his years of tuition, Antonia caught it with a marked expertise. She turned it in her palm, discovering it was masterfully carved of wood.

Michael lifted his hands in a gesture of surrender. "I deserve to die at your hands!" he declared.

She giggled in spite of herself. "Michael, you're so absurd!"

He smiled. "That's the first time you've called me Michael in three years."

She resumed a straight face. "I shouldn't have done so, m'lord," she said in prim tones. "'Twas presumptuous of me."

"Cut line, Antonia." His smile faded, and he raked a hand through his hair. "What was I supposed to do? You were only twelve when I left for Oxford.... Five years can do a lot towards changing a person." He took a turn about the room, slapping the sword against his palm, then turned, his gaze raking her from head to toe. With a heavy sigh, he resumed his pacing.

"I was a guest of Lord Hamsley the night his daughter sneaked uninvited into my room. I sent her away post-haste, whereupon she roused her parents, spouting utter lies. The little baggage was a consummate actress, swooning and feigning die-away airs, all the while accusing me of compromising her.

"'Twas an unpleasant scene. I refused to allow her to entrap me, and finally she broke, confessing her delicate condition." A grimace twisted his mouth. "They were full of apologies, and I must confess, I was incredibly sad for them all, though it made me mad as a hornet that she'd try and use me as her scapegoat. I repaired immediately to Montewilde Park for a reprieve."

He came to a halt less than a foot from her. A wry grin etched his mouth. "I don't normally allow my temper to run unchecked. But your antic, coming hot on the heels of hers—gads, she was only sixteen—was the proverbial straw. You were my Sissy-britches Annie, and . . . and I couldn't bear the thought that you might endure the pain and humiliation she was sure to." He swallowed hard. "I never really doubted your innocence, but you must admit, you were always rather wild. I couldn't trust that if you ran unchecked, you wouldn't land yourself in a scrape."

For long moments she stared into his eyes, careful to keep her emotions at bay. On one hand, she could accept his concern for the hoydenish girl she'd been; on the other, she could slap him for being so utterly blind to her motives. Even worse, for suspecting she might do the same with any man. But three years of schooling her feelings served her well. She inclined her head, acknowledging his explanation.

"I'm not sure you understand the extent of my frustration at the time... again, I apologize. For my nasty words, my harsh accusations... for tattling." He snorted and folded his arms. "I shouldn't have kissed you, either, but that's one action I'm not sure I wouldn't repeat."

His reminder of those moments she'd considered such heavenly bliss cracked her composure. Her lashes swooped down; she distrusted herself to speak.

He withdrew the sword from her unresisting fingers, and replaced both above the fireplace. "Antonia, I was a cad," he candidly confessed, leaning against the mantel. "But I had no intention of being forced into marriage against my will."

He still believed she'd set out to compromise him. Let him think what he liked; 'twas far less painful than confessing she'd loved him, and had only wanted him to return that love and seek her hand.

The ghost of a smile traced her lips. "It seems I must tender an apology of my own. I do so, m'lord. My actions were lamentable."

He inclined his head, whether in agreement or acceptance of her apology, she didn't know. A wicked gleam lit his eyes. "I propose then," he murmured, "that we kiss and make up."

Her lashes lowered and her gaze fell to his well-cut lips. Her smile was tremulous. "I daresay we needn't go that far, but I'm not averse to suspending hostilities."

"Ah," came Rodney's satisfied voice from the doorway. "Heard it with my own ears, Michael... suspending hostilities and all that. About blasted time, I'd say, and I won't let her renege on't." A playful grin touched his mouth and he crossed the room to pour a glass of wine.

"How long have you been there?" Antonia demanded.

"Since Michael suggested you kiss and make up. Was waiting to see if you'd take him up on his handsome offer." He chuckled unabashedly at her blush.

"And if I had?" came her cross query.

"I'd have enjoyed the scene immensely."

"Wretch."

CHAPTER SIX

WITH THE EVENING well under way, and two riderless horses secured to the coach, they started off, leaving two empty wine bottles in their wake. High spirits prevailed. Michael and Rodney sprawled comfortably on the seat opposite Antonia. She herself was in a benevolent mood, due to the amount of wine she'd consumed and the pleasurable company. Dinner had been thoroughly enjoyable. She'd forgotten how much she appreciated Michael—his lively wit, his keen intelligence, the slow smile which lent perfection to his handsome countenance.

"That's more fun than I've had in an age," she said with a happy sigh. "I rather wish we'd cried pax long ago, Michael. You're a most charming companion."

Michael sent her a sidelong glance and chuckled. "Remind me to feed you wine more often, Antonia. It does wonderful things for your disposition."

She gurgled appreciatively.

"Perfect thing, that," Rodney said. "Your calling truce, I mean. You must know, Antonia, Michael vowed he'd roast before he saw you wed to that pompous, posturing ass."

Antonia studied Michael quizzically from beneath half-lowered lids. What did he care?

Michael emitted a strangled oath. "Which words," he said in damping tones, "weren't meant to be repeated."

Antonia's delighted laugh rippled forth. "Behold my plotting partner. You must see, m'lord, how grossly the odds are stacked against me."

"What you need is a comrade-in-arms well versed in the art of intrigue." He gazed across at her, a soft gleam of challenge in his dark eyes.

"Who might you suggest?"

"I'd be more than happy to offer my services."

"None better," Rodney interjected.

Antonia nodded her head. "I gratefully accept your offer, m'lord. Three heads, after all, can only be better than two. I admit I'm at point non plus. The aforementioned pompous, posturing ass—" her eyes twinkled "—is removing to London. To press his suit, you see. So, I have to contend not only with the problem he presents, but with his own horrid self."

"Botheration!" Rodney expostulated. "He'll babble to all and sundry—I take it he's made his offer?"

She nodded. "And a pretty price he's willing to pay, I gather. Papa won't accept until the end of the Season."

"Much good that'll do," Rodney scoffed. "Wilson'll be sure to send your suitors to the roundabout. Once he mentions the sum he's offered, only lecherous old men willing to part with their gold will have the courage to face Father."

Michael noted Antonia's wide, sad eyes gazing into the blackness beyond the window. A qualm of repentance stirred within him. He'd experienced a lot of those in the past few days.

"I don't suppose treating him rudely would have any effect?" he asked gently.

Rodney snorted. "That man's tenacity is frightening. His blunt has paved the way, and there'll be no shaking him. He'll cling like a leech. The only way..."

"Yes?" Antonia prompted, her eyes lighting hopefully.

"The only way Lord Wilson will admit defeat is if you became engaged to another man." Rodney flashed a wide smile and snapped his fingers. "But that's it! A false engagement is the answer. Once he cries off, you can break it."

Michael came to attention, his heartbeat escalating.

"Simply said," Antonia scoffed. "Your drink has gone to your head, Brother."

"You said wealthy bachelors are hard to find. And you've but six weeks to bring one up to scratch. I think my idea would suffice."

She stared with helpless disbelief. "Who would I become engaged to? And suppose I do find a temporary fiancé. We break the engagement—what's one scandal more added to the list? Lord Wilson renews his offer, with not so generous a settlement, and I'm back where I started, minus the six-week reprieve.

"The man who imprudently plays our game will be sued by Papa for breach of promise, and we'll end up in worse case than before. Providing, of course, we could find a man rich enough to be accepted by Papa in the first place."

With a smug smile, Rodney waved a hand towards Michael. "Behold your betrothed, m'lady. He's perfect! He's already agreed to become your comrade-in-arms, and Father'd never sue him. Besides, if you broke off, there'd be no cause for a suit." He shrugged. "It might ultimately land us in the same pickle, but perhaps Lord Wilson may find another woman to replace you in his affections in the meantime."

Michael's mind raced. This was too good, too perfect, too *easy.* Bless Rodney's unsuspecting heart!

"Who'd have him?" Antonia queried with a shudder. She glanced at Michael, who was strangely still. Fearing this wasn't his idea of becoming a partner-in-intrigue, she shook her head. "We can't drag Michael into that sort of scheme, Rodney. There's no telling what the outcome would be. It's far too risky. Can you imagine the people we'd deceive, the *trouble* we could land in?"

Rodney shrugged and threw himself back against the seat.

"The idea does have merit," Michael quietly observed. "I think we should consider it."

Rodney again leaned forward, throwing Antonia a triumphant glance.

She shook her head helplessly. "It's a hare-brained notion, can't you see?" Her eyes pleaded with Rodney, then Michael. She spread her hands in helpless entreaty. "Michael, we've scarce spoken in three years, and suddenly—voila!—we're engaged? Just as Rodney breaks with an heiress? The entire ton knows the Earl of Montewilde has great expectations and the Marley family is deep in the suds! There wouldn't be a soul not chewing over that morsel! I don't care for the stigma, especially with the announcement of our broken engagement coming hot on its heels. Then won't the gossipmongers gloat."

"I can scarce credit you, Antonia!" Rodney snorted. "You'd greet that fleshy, ogling jackanapes at the altar rather than lose a little face? Are we talking of scandal, m'dear? You mention compromise, and then have the audacity to call *my* idea hare-brained? Hah!" His tones were eloquent with offended logic.

Michael waited with bated breath. He didn't dare add another word to Rodney's argument, lest he appear too eager.

Bowing her head, Antonia played with the strings of her reticule. Rodney spoke an abundance of truth, which wasn't easy to bear. The thought of entering a false engagement with Michael, however, was more than she'd reckoned on, though, strangely enough, she didn't doubt Michael approved the idea. Sensing his suppressed impatience as he awaited her answer, she released a long sigh.

"You're right. Having my name dragged through the mud would be preferable to marrying Lord Wilson."

Michael and Rodney breathed as one.

"Hopefully, we can circumvent even that," Michael said. "There are, as you say, some obstacles, but I can't see them causing undue problems."

He rubbed his hands together. "First, we'll have to be seen frequently in one another's company. Eyebrows may rise, but it shouldn't make for more than passing speculation. Given a couple weeks, we'll be so commonplace that interested onlookers will watch the *Gazette* for an announcement."

His smile flashed white in the soft lantern light. "Thus, the least of our problems is solved. Your father is our toughest proposition, for we can't know how he'll accept my suit." He lifted one shoulder in a shrug. "As I've yet to come into my inheritance, I can only guess the amount I'll receive. That leaves us with two options.

"I can go to him with my bogus offer, chancing his rejection on the grounds that he'd have to wait for the settlement, and that I might be unable to top Lord Wilson's offer. Or—and I feel this the best course of action—we can simply put the announcement in the *Gazette*. Once it's done, it's done." He shrugged eloquently. "Then we sit back and wait for the fireworks."

"Capital notion!" Rodney applauded.

Antonia shuddered. "Papa would be furious."

"True," Michael agreed. "I shouldn't like deceiving him."

"All's fair in love and war," was Rodney's stout decree.

Antonia smiled. "Mmm. Besides, he's schemed without a qualm to get the highest bidder for my hand. 'Tis only fair to use what devices I can to thwart his plans. Michael, I think that's the most likely solution." She paused. "But let's be prepared to face the consequences should they prove disastrous."

"Oh, doom and gloom, Antonia," Rodney chastised. "At worst, you two'll be forced to wed, and if you want my opinion—"

"I don't," she snapped, silencing him.

In one easy motion, Michael transferred himself to her seat. He gave her hand a comforting squeeze. "I know this isn't easy for you," he said softly. "I haven't exactly fostered your confidence in the past. But I promise to do my best to see you come to minimal harm.... Can you trust me in that, Antonia?"

She returned his searching gaze, a multitude of questions buzzing in her brain. As many scattered emotions chased about her heart. She was frightened to ask why he'd go to these lengths for her, and more apprehensive still that he'd pierce her guarded heart, leaving her to risk again the agonizing pain of his rejection. Finally, after long moments, she spoke. "I haven't any choice but to trust you, Michael."

With her life, she was sure she could. But with her heart?

LADY MATILDA HAWTHORNE reposed on a small, stuffed sofa. A grey-haired matron, pleasingly plump, she exuded an air of simple elegance manifested in the décor of her home, her tastefully cut robe and every movement she made. The three young people were shown into her yellow salon, and she didn't bother rising, merely laid aside her book. "So," she said, her eyes twinkling, "the prodigal has returned with his errant young sister. Michael, I didn't expect to see you."

Michael lifted the beringed hand she proffered. "Hallo, Matilda. I couldn't deny myself the honour of returning these two scapegraces to your loving care. Being at your door, I thought it best to see if I could smooth their paths as they seek to regain your good graces."

Matilda laughed, her gaze sweeping her charges. "And well they need it. You were in the country, too? I trust your journey was pleasant, and that you're aware Antonia's been laid up with a putrid sore throat for the past three days?"

"'Tis the word I received, m'lady," Michael returned with an appreciative chuckle. "I've great hopes she'll be recovered by morning. And yes, the company made my journey most pleasant, but since my horse awaits, I must bid you good night."

"I shan't detain you." She gave him a good-natured grin. "I must needs scold my charges, and that can't wait all night." The secret smiles on her charges' faces indicated they were indeed intimidated by their fierce aunt. "Shall we see you tomorrow?"

"Of an assurity," he promised. Turning to Antonia, he raised her hand to his lips, his fingers lingering round hers. He grinned whimsically and winked. Antonia smiled sweetly. Matilda's brows lifted in astonishment.

Michael left the salon, closing the door behind him. Only Parker was privileged to witness the exuberant fist he thrust in the air and the exultant "Yes!" that hissed from his lips. Parker passed him his gloves and saw him whistling out the door.

"Rodney," murmured his aunt, her eyes glued to her niece, "I shall speak with you in the morning. Good night, Nephew, and please tell Parker to bring tea."

"Yes, ma'am, and good night!" Rodney replied agreeably. He strode to the door, throwing his sister an encouraging nod as he withdrew.

"Your days in the country, it seems, have proved most interesting, Niece," Lady Hawthorne mused.

"Indeed, they have." Antonia set aside her reticule and plopped onto a comfortable chair with a full-blown sigh. "I really must apologize, Aunt Mattie—"

"Yes, yes." Matilda waved a bored hand. "I should ring you a peal, but I won't. I'm sure your father has taken care of that."

Antonia giggled in affirmation. Parker tapped discreetly on the door and entered with the tea-tray.

"Ah, Parker, set it here, and then you may retire." Parker deposited his offering on the low table she indicated and retreated without a sound.

"Now, m'dear," Matilda said, settling back with a cup of tea, "do tell. I've never seen you smile so sweetly at Michael, and I confess to being on tenterhooks."

"'Tis nothing so wonderful, Aunt." Antonia lifted a shoulder in a careless shrug. "We've merely agreed to suspend hostilities, which I'm convinced was long overdue. Michael's been most charming, and I'm inclined to renew our friendship."

"Most noble of you, I'm sure," Matilda commented drily. "I feel certain Michael's been waiting this age for your heart to soften."

"Did I sound stuffy?" Antonia asked, contrite. "I didn't mean to. And yes, he did seem rather eager to make amends."

"I'm delighted. I was convinced you two would stand at daggers drawn for the remainder of our lives. What a pleasant change it'll be to have you on speaking terms." Matilda gazed at her niece, her eyes lighting with humour. "I confess to some curiosity at your change of heart. You didn't receive a bump on the head while in the country, did you?"

Antonia giggled again, but sobered quickly. "I received the *most* unpalatable news. It's a rather long story, but..."

Matilda settled back onto her sofa, listening with feigned disinterest as her niece unfolded her tale. But when Antonia enlarged upon her father's plans for her future, she leaned forward, eyes wide with disbelief, and punctuated Antonia's story with remarks such as, "Lord Wilson? He surely can't be serious! He has windmills in his attic!"

"Well," she huffed after Antonia finished, "we'll see about that! If your own father has taken leave of his senses, it's left to me to protect you, and so I shall. He hasn't heard the end of this!"

"He gave me a letter for you." Antonia fished in her reticule for the missive. Matilda accepted it, tearing it open. She skimmed its contents, a frown creasing her brow.

"He's in a coil, indeed," she conceded. "But I can't countenance his solution. He bids me welcome Lord Wilson, and basically repeats what you've told me. Well, there's more than one way to skin a rat, m'dear, and never fear, it shall be done. You realize it'll likely end with that ultimate walk up the aisle, but be assured—" she wagged a finger "—it shan't be Lord Wilson who meets you at the altar."

Matilda drummed quick fingers upon the arm of the sofa, an action attesting to the mental activity behind her soft grey eyes. She smiled. "I congratulate you, Niece! Making amends with Michael is one of the brighter things I've known you to do! Even if he must wait a bit for the settlement—I've heard there's something irregular going on with old George's will—my brother cannot deny Michael is a more excellent match than Lord Wilson. I definitely wouldn't balk at having a countess in the family, and Montewilde Park far surpasses in grandeur that pretentious monstrosity of Lord Wilson's."

"Aunt," Antonia countered, "it's not my intention to bring Michael up to snuff, I assure you. Why, the thought never—" Matilda pierced her with keen grey eyes, and Antonia capitulated with a tiny shrug. "He is preferable to Lord Wilson. I couldn't allow any old tiff to stand in the way of a possible parti, but Aunt, I pray he never gets the slightest inkling of my motives being less than pure."

"My dear niece, do you take me for a gapeseed? You think I'd dream of ruining your chances with him? My darling girl, I shall promote your case at every turn. Should I find him in your bedchamber, I'd turn a blind eye!"

Antonia laughed, knowing what a stickler Matilda was for convention. "I thank you, Aunt," she stated, "but I shouldn't rely on that outcome. There's no telling what may happen...." Inwardly, she chafed at her forced deceit. What a tangled web they'd woven. Aunt Mattie would be in alt when she and Michael announced their engagement, and deflated when they broke it.

"Mmm," agreed Matilda, tapping her finger against her chin. "Alex Harvey called on you the day you hied yourself off to the country. I told him you were ill, and he's been back both days since, wishing you a quick recovery. Those flowers are for you."

"For me? From Mr. Harvey?" Antonia rose to inspect the pretty collection, which was larger than the norm. "How strange," she murmured, fingering the card.

"Why so?"

"Well, to be sure, he's invited me for an occasional drive and we dance regularly, but I don't recall sensing any real solicitude for me.... But you say he called three times?"

"He seems quite eager that I convey his regards."

"Kind of him," Antonia acknowledged, leaning forward to sniff the bouquet. "They're lovely."

"Yes...he's a personable young man, Antonia. Quite handsome, with an excellent taste in attire. His background is highly respectable, his pockets fairly well-lined, and he has great expectations."

"Don't they all?" Antonia returned with a sniff. Alex Harvey was all her aunt described. Although not precisely dashing, he was a man most young ladies would feel privileged to win. She'd never consider herself among them. "I'm not sure I should like to marry him, Aunt."

"I'm not suggesting you marry him, Antonia. But if Michael has serious intentions in your direction, Harvey would be the perfect man to bring him round—if you catch my meaning. And if I were you, I'd nab the Earl of Montewilde in a trice."

Trailing up to bed, Antonia was busy with other ideas. Could she place Alex in her affections? Anything would be better than being vulnerable to Michael. Their forced proximity over the next weeks would be trial enough. Already she imagined him as her groom, and such a silly notion wouldn't suffice. 'Twas merely chivalrous instinct which demanded he come to her aid. She required a defence against him, and perhaps Alex was the solution. Unless, of course, she stood a chance of bringing Michael round.

Mercy, she didn't know what to do.

CHAPTER SEVEN

MICHAEL ENTERED the breakfast parlour at the unseemly hour of ten. Well used to running tame in Matilda's home, he divested himself of hat and gloves and greeted the family cheerily.

"Help yourself, Michael," Matilda offered, waving a hand towards the sideboard. "You're just in time."

"Thank you, I hoped I would be. I left the house rather early and didn't want to bother waiting for breakfast." He secured a plate and filled it, casting a sideways glance at Antonia as she hovered between muffins or toast. "I trust the morning finds you well, Antonia?" he asked with a crooked grin, spearing a thick slice of ham.

"Perfectly," Antonia purred, deciding on the muffin. Covertly she studied his trim, lithe figure, noting the wide shoulders, slender hips and muscular legs. Most handsome, she concluded, not for the first time. Dare she try and bring him about as her aunt had suggested?

"Good, then perhaps you'd care to drive with me this afternoon?"

Antonia hauled her thoughts into line, tore her gaze from his sun-bronzed throat, and stared blankly.

"Of course she would," Matilda crowed from behind her. "An afternoon in the Park will be just the thing for her."

Antonia caught the question in Michael's eyes. "I'd be pleased to," she said demurely, turning quickly lest he see the blush staining her cheeks. She ignored Matilda's swift frown and applied herself to her meal.

"Michael, I'm delighted you and Antonia have chosen to lay aside your differences. I've been so hard put assuring you two weren't placed at the same whist table or forced to speak with each other for more than a moment." Matilda gave a complacent smile. "I may give a dinner party just for the sake of not having to manoeuvre you to opposite ends of the table!"

Michael chuckled. "It'll be a change, eh?" He chose the chair beside Antonia's, and sat down, his thigh brushing against hers. "Shall we practice, to be sure we can behave ourselves through an entire meal?"

Matilda smiled. Antonia blushed even more deeply, but said nothing.

"Rodney, however, is a different matter," said Matilda, sending the young man a sidelong glance. "I haven't pried a word from him. I've never seen the boy so reticent."

"Because I'm mad as a hornet, Aunt, and don't trust myself to speak of it," her nephew replied with a dark scowl. "Michael may tell you."

"Seems Maria accused him of being a fortune-hunter," Michael quietly supplied. Another qualm, sharper now, pierced him.

The ladies gasped as one.

"Turned on me like a viper," Rodney grunted, staring into the depths of his coffee cup. "Makes me so blasted angry she could even think it, much less voice such a slur to my integrity. Now Father's queer start has put paid to any chance of reconciliation. One word of this business reaches her ears, and I'll be branded a fortune-hunter for the rest of my days."

Michael winced and reached for his coffee.

"Rodney, I feel so ashamed," cried Antonia. "I've been so busy bemoaning my own predicament, and yours has been unbearable. Can I help?" She felt the veriest beast, castigating *him* for breaking off with his heiress.

Rodney laughed harshly. "I fear there's no help for it."

"We are in a pickle," pronounced Matilda. "But I've never known a Marley to bow to slander. We'll come about, never you fear. You'll not be branded a fortune-hunter, and I'll see Antonia marry one of the richest purses in the kingdom. Hurry, Niece. We must ready ourselves for a shopping expedition. It won't do for you to be seen in the Park before it's announced you're well again."

"Yes, Aunt," Antonia replied, finishing her coffee.

Michael gave mute thanks that none of them noticed his silence. Rodney loved Maria, that much was clear. But what was he to do? If they reconciled before he secured Antonia, he could kiss his own fortune goodbye. But what if, because of him, they never did?

MATILDA'S CARRIAGE turned into Bond Street. She cast a critical eye upon her niece, clad in an icy-blue gown. "Oh mercy, you look rather too healthy, Antonia. Do keep your handkerchief at hand, and cough just the teeniest bit into it at intervals. And my dear," she adjured, "when Michael asks you to go driving, for heaven's sake, don't act as if it's a sacrifice! You needn't play missish games. Perk up, and let him know you'd absolutely kill for the chance!"

A bubble of laughter escaped Antonia. "Surely, Aunt, that's doing it too brown?"

"However, you take my meaning."

"Yes," Antonia assured her, eyes twinkling.

"Good." Matilda rapped a signal to the coachman. "We're in luck. There's Mrs. Bryson. We can rely on her to announce to all that you're well. We'll speak with her for a moment."

"Ah, she's entering the milliner's," Antonia replied with satisfaction. "My bonnet should be repaired by now. How was the picnic, by the by?"

"A bore. Nothing more untoward happened than Mrs. Martin's dowdy daughter spilling punch on her hideous orange gown. She thought it a Cheltenham tragedy; I considered it a blessing. Now, do you need another bonnet, perchance?"

"If you're coughing up the dibs," Antonia answered brightly as she was being helped down, "I could use two."

"Antonia!" exclaimed Matilda, halting in mid-step. "Wherever did you hear such cant?"

"From Rodney, of course."

"You know a lady doesn't use such language. For that, you shall only get one."

"Yes, Aunt," Antonia humbly agreed with a wide grin.

Matilda cast her a withering glance. "You're a wretch, young lady. Lord Wilson should thank me for saving him from wedding you. Now, let's find that bonnet, and remember, just a tiny cough."

LATER THAT AFTERNOON, Antonia breezed into the drawing-room, clad in a striped confection of magenta and white. She'd shunned a parasol in favour of her new chip straw bonnet trimmed with magenta ribbon and a small spray of flowers. She placed it on the hall table, where she could conveniently regain it. Her drive with Michael would commence after tea, and she disliked making him wait.

Matilda was conversing with her bosom friend, Mrs. Hadley. Michael and Rodney lounged at ease, and Antonia saw at a glance that today's tea would be quite informal. She basked in Michael's appreciative look, feeling unaccountably shy.

Mrs. Hadley claimed her attention. "I'm glad to see you well again, Antonia dear," she said with a sweet smile. "I hope you are completely recovered?"

"Thank you, I am." Mrs. Hadley no doubt knew the whole of the story, seeing as how she and Matilda were close as inkelweavers. Antonia secured tea and a macaroon, and chose a chair. "How are you today, Mrs. Hadley?"

"Enjoying good health and a coze with your aunt, as usual."

"Mr. Alex Harvey," Parker intoned from the door.

Alex strode towards them. Antonia sent him a bright smile, taking careful note of his handsome figure in buff-coloured breeches and a superfine coat. He greeted the older ladies first, and she remarked his perfect manners. The men he saluted less warmly. To her surprise, Antonia detected a hostile note in his manner towards Michael. The warm concern filling his eyes a moment later convinced her she was mistaken.

"I'm pleased to see you enjoying good health once again, Miss Marley." He smiled, bowing over her hand. "Did your aunt tell you I called?"

"She did, and I thank you for your concern." She gave him a sweet smile. "The flowers are lovely."

"I hoped they might brighten the dreary hours in the sickroom." He thanked Matilda for the cup of tea she proffered, and took a seat beside Antonia.

"They did indeed," she answered tongue-in-cheek, thankful they weren't taking tea in the yellow salon, where he'd be privileged to see his posy hadn't made it to the sickroom.

His gaze swept over her with decided approval. "You look enchanting," he murmured. "Will you honour me with a drive in the Park this afternoon?"

"Oh, dear. I'm already promised to drive with Lord Alton. I thank you anyway." When her eyes communicated that she wasn't averse to his suggestion, Michael frowned, and Alex sent him a daggered glance.

"I'm sorry to hear that, for my own selfish reasons. You'll be the loveliest lady in the Park today, I make no doubt." His smile caressed her. "May I drive you tomorrow?"

"I should be pleased," she returned with a winning smile.

Michael frowned again, in counterpart to Alex's gleeful grin. Though baffling, the situation was somewhat amusing.

She chatted with Alex whilst he finished his tea. He returned his cup to the tray, spoke politely to Matilda, and bid the ladies good day. To the gentlemen, he executed a slight bow. Lifting Antonia's hand, he touched his lips to her fingers. "Until tomorrow. I look forward to it with great pleasure."

She inclined her head, smiling. "Good day, Mr. Harvey." She watched his retreating form, finding nothing to fault.

"Antonia, do you care for more tea?" Matilda's question brought her attention round. She passed her cup, peeking across at Michael. Her brow wrinkled at the scowl he directed at his boots. Rodney studied her, frowning. What was up with them? Were they angry at the attention she accorded Alex? She lifted her cup, thinking it a most curious situation.

"MICHAEL, IS THIS your new team?" Antonia asked, admiring the pair of matched greys standing docilely with

Hammond, his groom, at their heads. "They're beautiful!"

"Mmm," Michael agreed with unconcealed pride. "I got such a bargain I couldn't pass them up. They're sweet goers, and though they don't look it now, they do have a bit of spunk in their bones."

"Is this your first time in the Park with them?"

"Yes." His hand closed lightly over hers, and he handed her onto the seat of his phaeton. Settling beside her, he took up the reins. "Hammond brought them up just yesterday morning, so this will be the first time anyone's seen them. Like as not, we'll be accosted several times before making one round—which I'm hoping you won't mind, as it'll suit our purposes admirably."

Hammond took his position at the rear of the phaeton; Michael lifted the reins and clucked. The greys moved into a trot, their hooves clipping smartly against the cobblestones.

"And so the charade begins," Antonia murmured.

Michael threw her a swift glance, frowning. "It needn't be a total farce, Antonia. We're working to see you don't wed Lord Wilson, and if we play our parts well, we'll succeed. Don't concern yourself unduly. It could be a lark, leading Society about by the ear." With a finger under her chin he tilted her face up to his. "And if we could reclaim our former friendship," he murmured, "'twould be reward enough for me."

Though his gaze didn't waver, she was prey to tumultuous emotions. Love, yearning, anger, hurt... his warm breath fanned her cheek, sending a pleasant shiver down her spine. She pulled in a breath, her lashes falling. "I can't like deceiving Aunt Mattie."

"I don't like deceiving anyone, but sometimes 'tis necessary. Circumstances can force people into doing what they'd rather not." He turned into the Park gates with an encouraging smile. "So, shall we do the pretty, and for the time being forget about plots, Aunt Mattie, and Lord Wilson?"

"Halloo there!" came a voice from their left.

Antonia choked. "Easier said than done, m'lord. Lord Wilson, how... nice to see you."

"A surprise too, I'll wager," he returned jovially. "I'm certain you didn't expect to see me here." He chuckled, sending her a conspiratory wink. "I've come a-courtin', m'girl. Got your papa's consent, you know." He gave a self-important nod, his eyes conveying the great honour he bestowed on her, before he flicked a glance towards Michael. "M'lord, I'll thank you to remember that."

"The course of true love ne'er did run smoothly," was Michael's enigmatic response.

"Heh, heh. Quite so," agreed Lord Wilson, eyeing him with uncertainty.

"Ah, Sir Lawrence Halverson is beckoning. A good day to you, Lord Wilson." With a smart click, Michael urged his team forward.

Antonia waved her fingers in farewell, laughing. "It'll take him a while to understand about the course of love."

Michael smiled. "I fear quick wits aren't numbered amongst his strong suits."

"Mmm," she gurgled, casting a glance to the rear. "He's following us!" she hissed, clutching his arm.

Michael groaned. "You're bamming me."

"No. That cerise waistcoat is unmistakable."

Michael laughed. "Neither is subtlety one of his virtues. At least we'll have no difficulty knowing how our opponent stands... and where, at all times." He halted beside a group of young men, nodding a greeting. "Lawrie, good to see you... gentlemen."

"Michael," returned Sir Lawrence, "...Miss Marley." His assessing glance flicked over the two of them, his brows rising a fraction. "Allow me to introduce my companions. My cousins, Frederick and Albert Halverson."

Greetings exchanged, Sir Lawrence asked, "How goes Rodney, Miss Marley?"

"In need of support, I fear." She gave a slight grimace.

"Then I shall call upon him." Lawrie's good-natured grin creased his boyishly handsome face. "New bloods, Michael? Very nice." His approving gaze travelled over their trim lines. "Any more where they came from?"

"Sorry. I shan't even tell you what I paid for them—I dislike seeing my friends turn green." A quick grin split Michael's face.

"Figures," Lawrie grunted. His gaze moved to the rear of Michael's phaeton, where the noses of Lord Wilson's team nudged an uncomfortable Hammond. "Quite an entourage you have with you today."

"Yes...and if you'd kindly compliment him on his waistcoat, I'd be much obliged. Be sure to ask him the direction of his tailor, and keep him occupied a *long* time."

Lawrie's eyes lighted with mischief. "Be happy to. Good day, Michael...Miss Marley." Drawing a quizzing glass from his pocket, he turned his horse about. "Sir! A most stunning waistcoat!"

Chuckling, Michael and Antonia moved on. Moments later, Mrs. Bryson accosted them, her thin, reedy voice piercing their quiet harmony.

"Lord Alton! What a pleasure," she shrilled. "And oh, my, if it isn't Miss Marley!"

Her thin grey hair was scraped away from her narrow face into a tight bun. A grey merino walking dress accented the angular lines of her figure. Michael and Antonia greeted her, their tones polite but lacking warmth.

"What a coincidence to see you twice in one day, Miss Marley," Mrs. Bryson observed with a toothy smile. "I've seen and heard so much of you today. La, it quite boggles my senses. Lord Delbert Wilson is in Town.... I saw him but a moment ago and he informs me he's come to court you." She gave a grating titter, dipping her parasol coyly. "Lucky girl. And now driving with Montewilde. It's not nice of you to steal all the beaux. My, won't the Honourable Lucy Davenport be dismayed!"

"I can't conceive why she should be," Michael said drily.

"La, m'boy, you must know her mother's angled for your title this last age."

"Then surely 'tis her mother who'll be disappointed. My team is become restive, Mrs. Bryson. You'll forgive us if we move on?"

"Of course." Her toothy smile swallowed her face again, and she waved them onward with a mercenary gleam in her eyes.

"I can't like that woman," Antonia said, shaking her head.

"A most unlikable creature," Michael agreed. "She covets gossip like a miser covets gold. What a wealth of information she's gleaned today. She'll be hoarse before the sun sets."

"Mmm. And the Marley's are the current on dit... causing quite a stir, aren't we?"

"But again, it suits us admirably. We can safely trust in Mrs. Bryson to lay our groundwork." He chuckled. "Lady Davenport will be cross as crabs."

"Michael... I hadn't considered you might have emotional attachments elsewhere. Are you sure we should continue?"

He snorted. "You think my motives entirely unselfish? Lucy Davenport's heart won't be broken, I assure you. Her ambitions may receive a setback, but I doubt she'll be prostrate with grief. Mayhap she'll be more subtle in her attempts to learn the worldly value of her next victim." He smiled mockingly. "And now, though I hesitate to ask you to commit a faux pas, would you be pleased to glance behind? I'd like to know where our erstwhile hound is."

Antonia laughed and peeked over her shoulder. "He's a few carriages back, craning his neck this way and that—searching for us, I presume. I'm afraid he doesn't look too pleased."

"I somehow didn't expect him to."

CHAPTER EIGHT

"MR. HARVEY," Antonia greeted that young man the next afternoon, struck again by his pristine appearance. Not a hair was disturbed, and she vowed a wrinkle wouldn't dare mar the elegance of his blue superfine coat. She was thankful she'd taken pains to ensure her hair was neatly coiffed, and that her white muslin gown was the first stare of fashion.

"I'm dreadfully sorry to keep you waiting, but Aunt Mattie insisted we go shopping, and we found ourselves in the greatest tangle of traffic. We arrived home quite an hour later than expected. . . ." She spread her hands. "I do apologize."

"Don't concern yourself, Miss Marley." Alex lifted her hand to his lips, gazing fervently into her eyes. "To behold your beauty is worth any wait I've endured. You look stunning . . . as usual."

"Thank you." She dimpled up at him, her usual method of dealing with fulsome, and sometimes insincere, compliments, which she rarely let go to her head.

"Shall we then?" he murmured, offering his arm. "It's been this age since I've had the pleasure of your company. I fear I've neglected you dreadfully, but with that puppy Smythe squiring you about so fastidiously, little room has been left for your other admirers."

"I hadn't realized I was in such great demand."

"Therein lies one of your sweetest charms. Your modesty is most appealing." He assisted her to the phaeton's seat, squeezing her hand ever so gently. She thought the action rather familiar, but didn't protest. When he swung up beside her and took the reins, she noted immediately that he hadn't Michael's light-handed skill with the ribbons.

"Now, tell me why we've never dispensed with formality and called each other by our given names." He flashed her a charming smile, and urged his team into a trot.

"How remiss of us. We must remedy that with all haste."

"My sentiments exactly. For though 'Miss Marley' has a certain flavour, there's no denying 'Antonia' is by far the more appealing. In my opinion, 'tis the perfect name for you . . . are you aware it means 'inestimable, priceless'?"

"Why, no! Thank you kindly, Alex," she replied, flattered. "I doubt my parents considered that, as I'm named after my father. It pleases me you find it a fitting name."

He captured her hand, drawing it to his lips. "I'm glad. I'd do anything to please you." He quirked a grin. She marvelled she'd never seen this gallant side, and found she liked him the better for it. However, she was rather puzzled at his sudden onslaught of charm.

Antonia wasn't surprised to find Lord Wilson hovering inside the Park gates, waiting to swoop upon her. Noting her escort, he checked himself with a frown. Realizing he couldn't like approaching a man he hadn't met, Antonia gave Alex a winning smile and dipped her parasol to obscure Lord Wilson from view.

Short minutes later, Alex clucked with annoyance. "Who's that dratted man following us?"

Antonia choked back a laugh. "Is he rather plump and does his attire remind you of a parrot?"

"Exactly so! The muzzles of his team are like to upset my groom."

"Oh, dear," Antonia sighed. The situation was almost comical. "That's Lord Wilson. He considers himself a contender for my hand, and like as not, will make a spectacle of himself in his attempts to win me."

"The deuce you say!" Alex expostulated. "You're bamming."

"I'm completely in earnest."

He glanced at her, shocked, then swivelled round to take closer inspection. "But he's fifty if he's a day!"

"No, actually," she disagreed placidly, "his age is nearer six and forty. He's very wealthy."

His brows rose in disbelief. "Which fact gives him the audacity to suppose he has a chance to win your hand?"

"It does if my father has encouraged him to believe such," she replied, affecting a careless shrug.

"'Sdeath," he breathed. "Do you say he's already offered for you?"

She nodded.

"How can your father contemplate such a match?"

"As I've said, he's fabulously wealthy, and from what I understand, prepared to be quite generous."

"'Sdeath," he muttered again, looking almost sick and even a trifle angry.

"Oh, pray don't concern yourself on my behalf," Antonia pleaded. "I'd supposed you already knew, as Mrs. Bryson was one of the first persons he told. Do I take it she's failed to make the business known to all of London? My, my, she's slipping."

"That woman!" Alex snorted. "I make it my business to steer as clear of her as may be."

"Yes? Then you'd best step up the pace. She's just ahead, watching us with avid interest. She'll detain us if given the chance."

Alex clicked to his team and Antonia waved her fingers as they passed by.

"Naughty girl, Miss Marley," the older woman twittered to the retreating phaeton.

"What did she mean by that?" Alex muttered, scowling.

"Aside from Lord Wilson, she saw me driving yesterday with Michael and now with you. She thinks I'm out to capture all the eligible partis. 'Tis what one expects of her mean mentality."

He considered her, a tiny line of concern etching his brow. "Mmm. Is Montewilde aware of Lord Wilson's...er, attachment?"

"A most apt description, Alex," she giggled. "Lord Wilson followed us about in like fashion yesterday. I'll soon be forced to forgo driving in the Park, lest I find myself caricatured in a cartoon depicting Lord Wilson forever on my heels. And yes, Michael knows."

"Has he promised to take an offer to your father to save you from that ill-favoured oaf?"

The question was calm, mildly curious, but Antonia noted tension in the tightening of his jaw. Her brows lifted a fraction. "Of course not," she said, a trifle more sharply than intended. "He's not able to top such an offer."

Alex relaxed and smiled apologetically. "Forgive me, Antonia. It's not my way to pry, but I confess to some concern for your plight. Had you already found a solution, I'd have bowed out and not concerned myself with how best to help you."

"How kind of you," she murmured contritely. Her hand touched his sleeve. "I didn't mean to be sharp, and really, you mustn't concern yourself. I'm firmly decided against marrying him, no matter what Papa says. Indeed, Lord Wilson is nothing more than a botheration, and I'm able to survive that." She gazed at him earnestly, feeling rather dishonest for not explaining that she did have a solution. He inclined his head, and she graced him with a sunny smile.

Straightening, she found herself under the regard of Lord Michael Alton, Rodney, Sir Lawrence and his cousins. She smiled and waved, noting the tight line of Michael's mouth and the worried glint in his eyes. Instantly, he nodded a greeting, his sensuous lips lifting in a smile. He urged his mount forward.

"Antonia." His gaze slid to her companion; he nodded and returned his attention to her. "I see you brought your chaperon along again. Shall we rid you of him?"

"I'd be most grateful."

Their gazes meshed, and held. He wheeled his black about. "Very well. Good day."

Alex urged his team on, sparing scarcely a nod of farewell to the men about to accost Lord Wilson.

"Forgive my curiosity, Alex," Antonia said, her tone puzzled. "But, being cousins, you and Michael don't seem to get on very well."

His smile was grim. "We're not cousins. We merely have family connexions."

"I see," she mused, and thought it prudent not to pursue the subject. He and Michael seemed to wish each other halfway round the world.

Michael watched Alex's phaeton blending with the mass of carriages and riders. Blast Harvey's eyes! Antonia hadn't rested her hand on *his* arm yesterday. And she hadn't charmed him with so winning a smile.

THE NEXT AFTERNOON, Mr. Berkley entered the yellow salon. He paused on the threshold, fidgeting with his fob watch. "Forgive me, ladies," he said, "for intruding upon you like this."

"Nonsense, Gerard." Lady Hawthorne motioned him to a chair with a wave of one beringed hand. "You're just in time to take tea, and we'd be pleased for your company."

"Thank you, Matilda." He expelled a long sigh, relaxing visibly, and moved to the chair she indicated. "Miss Marley, a pleasure to see you."

"And you, Mr. Berkley," Antonia responded, returning his smile. Maria's father was a distinguished-looking gentleman in his late forties, with kind eyes and greying hair. What Antonia most admired about him was his utter lack of pretence. None of the opulent wealth he possessed was displayed in either his manner or dress.

"I admit to being uncertain of my reception, Matilda." He accepted a cup of tea with a wry grin.

"You must know my house is always open to you, Gerard, and if our youngsters must squabble, I only hope it'll cause no hard feelings between us."

"My sentiments exactly." He made himself more comfortable on his chair. "I'm gratified you introduced the topic of our youngsters. They're the precise purpose of my visit."

"Shall I leave you two to chat?" Antonia asked.

"No. Please, Miss Marley, I'd have you stay if you don't mind."

"Certainly," she consented, her curiosity piqued.

She and Matilda waited expectantly as he sipped his tea, a frown furrowing his brow. "Can I hope this break between Rodney and Maria has distressed you as greatly as it has myself?"

Matilda sniffed delicately. "You'd have but to live with my nephew, Gerard, to know it has. He's been in the deepest of mopes, definitely out of sorts."

"I hope you won't find me lacking in sensibilities, but I'm relieved to hear that," he said, his expression changing to satisfaction. "I'd feared he might find himself well rid of her. Maria's been acting out of sorts as well, though she hotly denies it's anything to do with their break-up."

He shook his head fondly. "Little termagant. Can't say I blame Rodney for ending it. Any man with an ounce of character would've done the same. Rodney was quite civil about the entire affair, I hasten to add." He gave a sheepish chuckle. "In case you wonder how I came to know that...I listened at the door. Felt like a common servant, don't you know," he confessed, a mischievous light dancing in his eyes.

The ladies laughed. "What I wonder," Matilda mused, "is that she'd accuse him of being a fortune-hunter now, after nearly a year of engagement."

"And well you might. I was dumbfounded when I heard her spouting such nonsense." He rubbed his chin in contemplation. "Methinks there's mischief afoot."

"How so?" was Matilda's interested query.

Mr. Berkley sighed. "There's a certain young man Maria associated with when she was younger. I never liked him above half, but he was kind to Maria. Being an only child, her life, I fear, has been rather lonely, so I never saw fit to deny her his friendship.

"The man is a ne'er-do-well. When he left for the Continent, I can't say I was dismayed. I was pleased Maria settled on Rodney before he returned. The man's a crafty devil, and though I see him for the fortune-hunter he is, Maria, I'm afraid, is still quite innocent, and not so worldly-wise."

"You think this young man has been carrying tales?" asked Matilda.

"I have my suspicions," he agreed. "Since the break-up, he's been Maria's constant consoler. There's nothing he can't do for her. Thus, my dilemma. Maria refuses to hear any evil spoken against him, and stubbornly resists any attempts I make to learn why she accused Rodney of coveting her gold."

"Do we know this young man?" Antonia asked.

"I believe you know him rather well, Miss Marley. That's why I desired your audience. I had hopes you might shed some light on the subject." When she raised her brows in mute enquiry, he said simply, "Morton Smythe."

Her mouth gaped in shock, her face the picture of injured indignity. "Why, that rat! I've been so busy I scarce noticed his defection. Hardly flattering, since he's courted me assiduously these past four months. Oh, Mr. Berkley, I'd no notion he was using me. He seemed so genuine, so lacking in pretence."

"Mmm. Then you can understand why I'm at pains to see Maria come to her senses. I've no desire to come the heavy hand with her, but neither will I condone a match between them. I trust him so little, I have a man following her. It sounds almost Gothic, but I've no other course of action." He rubbed a weary hand over his face, sighing heavily.

"I consider that prudent, Gerard," Matilda assured him. She glanced at her niece. "Although I couldn't like saying it, I never trusted him, either. I know Rodney holds him in extreme disaffection."

"My affections were never engaged, Aunt," Antonia defended. "I merely found him an . . . amusing companion."

"Now that you're aware he cultivated you for his own underhanded purposes?" queried Mr. Berkley.

"I'm highly indignant! Were I a man, I'd call him out."

"Antonia," her aunt murmured repressively.

"I'm most vexed, Aunt. How dare he use me so wickedly? Maria could scarce disbelieve any tales he took to her, he's been so frequently in my company. Like as not, she'd assume he and I were quite the boon companions! He's used me to drive a shaft between her and Rodney, and I find that repugnant!"

"Mr. Smythe is unscrupulous, Miss Marley. He has indeed abused your friendship," Mr. Berkley said sympathetically. "We're left to discover if he's guilty, though I have little doubt he is. Tell me, did he show any untoward interest in their relationship?"

Antonia frowned in concentration. "Certainly he showed an interest, but I never considered his questions out of line. He did remark that Rodney must be pleased to make such a financially brilliant match. I took no umbrage, merely agreeing 'twas well she had a few pennies to clink together as Rodney certainly had none. I'm sorry, I didn't think my words would be misconstrued."

"You couldn't know he was up to mischief," Mr. Berkley said. "However, you may be able to help. You and Maria seemed to be on good terms. Perhaps you could speak with her, discover what's set her off?"

Antonia grimaced. "Maria cut me quite firmly the other day. I doubt she'll welcome me into her salon."

Mr. Berkley rolled his eyes in defeat. "That child! I apologize. She's in quite a taking over this. Miss Marley, be assured if you choose to call, you shan't be refused admittance into *my* home."

"Thank you, Mr. Berkley. I promise to do what I can." Maybe, if relations between Rodney and Maria were smoothed, her father would forget his ridiculous notion of wedding her to Lord Wilson. She and Michael could stop plotting...which could only make for more heartache. Who was she kidding? He was still the only man she wanted to marry, and the one man she'd least likely catch.

"Thank you. Ladies, I pray you won't consider me a meddling old man, but I desire to see my daughter happy."

"Of course you do," Matilda replied. "Maria's fortunate to have a father so concerned for her welfare. We'd all like to see her and Rodney reunited, and please, if we can be of further assistance, don't hesitate to ask."

"Very well. Let's hope for a quick resolution to this affair." He beamed a warm smile upon them, and rose, returning his cup to the tray. "I bid you good day; I've taken far too much of your time already."

"You'll keep us informed?" asked Matilda.

"Of an assurity."

His farewell bow was interrupted as Rodney, a thunderous scowl on his face, stalked into the room. He checked, stiffening perceptibly when he saw their visitor.

"Rodney!" Mr. Berkley's voice suffused with warmth, and he stepped forward to greet him. "Good to see you, m'boy."

"Mr. Berkley," Rodney returned warily, thawing somewhat under his kind regard. "Good to see you, too."

"I was on my way out, but please, feel free to call upon me any time. My house is always open to you."

Rodney was no proof against his earnest offer. The trace of a smile lifted his lips. "Thank you, sir. Perhaps I shall."

"I look forward to it," Mr. Berkley said, nodding. "Good day to you."

"Good day, sir." Rodney waited for the door to close before throwing himself onto a chair. "You won't guess who tooled Maria through the Park today," he said scathingly.

"Morton Smythe, perhaps?" Antonia asked sweetly.

CHAPTER NINE

"BLACKGUARD! VILLAIN!" Rodney muttered, his tones savage. He adopted a pugilistic stance in the middle of the drawing-room floor. Fists jabbing the air, he grunted, "I'll draw his cork. I'll make his blood flow—I'll give him no quarter. He'll be sorry he thought to cross swords with me. I'll beat his wretched hide to a pulp."

The news of Mr. Smythe's treachery had been imparted to him and Michael moments earlier. The ladies had considered it prudent to keep their knowledge close until they'd enjoyed the evening meal. Michael's arrival seconds after Mr. Berkley's departure made the feat feasible, as he'd immediately whisked Rodney away to join the fellows at White's. He'd accepted Matilda's invitation to return for dinner, making the meal a highlight in Antonia's eyes.

"Steady on, Rodney," Michael cautioned, draping a lazy arm over the back of the sofa he and Antonia shared. "We must do this thing in style, you know. I can arrange a meeting at Gentleman Jackson's."

"Only after the Duchess of Leavenworth's ball," Matilda decreed.

"And not until we've established his guilt," added Antonia.

"I've no doubt he's guilty," Rodney stated with conviction, dropping his stance and regaining his chair. "What I can scarce credit is she believed him. Well, she'll not find me waiting with open arms once she's discovered his duplicity."

Antonia exchanged a doubtful glance with her aunt. "You mustn't judge her too harshly, Rodney. After all, Morton can be quite convincing, and they were friends long before she met you."

"I've never given her cause to doubt my integrity," Rodney maintained in stout tones. "She knew I was top over tail—" he coloured, uncomfortably adjusting his position. "Accepting his word over mine is an insult I don't take kindly to."

"It's certainly not a tasty morsel to swallow," said Matilda sympathetically, "but sometimes one must forgive, lest one sacrifices one's future happiness." She bent over her needlework, fussing with a knot in the silk.

Rodney frowned and studied his nails.

Antonia considered her aunt's words, absently smoothing her hair as she did so. To her surprise, her fingers made warm contact with Michael's, and his quickly closed round hers. Strong and firm, they laced with hers in a startlingly intimate manner. Eyes wide, she swivelled to meet his gaze, finding lazy, drooping lids concealing his expression. His lips quirked into a teasing grin; he chuckled softly and released her hand.

A soft glow infused her; her lashes fell, and she folded her hands primly in her lap. Moments later, she again noted a slight disturbance with her hair. A finger, as feathery light as a breath, traced her neck from hairline to collar. She was unprepared for the tremor of delight which shivered down her spine, and again her startled gaze flew to Michael's. Humour sparkled from his eyes.

Cocky, impertinent man! Nonchalantly, she reached behind her, capturing his hand and manoeuvring it, unresisting, to his side. Purposefully her thumb rubbed along his palm as she once again released it, this time with a warning tap.

Michael drew a steadying breath. His grin faded and his eyes darkened as he expelled it in a long, soundless whistle. He regarded her without faltering, one corner of his mouth quirking upward in resolution. "Would you like to take a stroll through the garden, Antonia?" he drawled.

A smile touched her lips. He wasn't going to let it lie. She opened her mouth to inform him she was quite comfortable where she was—

"I'm sure she'd be delighted, Michael," Matilda chimed. "'Tis a lovely evening."

Antonia raised inquisitive brows towards her aunt, receiving a mild, vacant look in return, before Matilda returned her attention to her stitchery. Michael stood and reached for her hand, an unmistakable challenge lurking in his eyes as he led her out the garden door.

"Your impudence, sir, is astonishing," she said in her primmest tones as they traversed a path of the well-ordered garden. He was playing a game and she was going to match him, giving as much as she got.

"Mmm," he agreed, "and unequaled by any but your own. Were I another man, I'd be tempted to an action such as this...." His finger tipped up her chin, and he lowered his head, taking her lips in a soft, lingering kiss.

"But since I'm not..." He swept her to him, and claimed her mouth in a gently searching, exquisitely provocative kiss. His tongue traced her parted lips and she shuddered with delight, losing herself in his heady embrace. When he drew her more closely to the taut strength of his frame, she revelled in his warmth. The words 'I love you' trembled on her lips.

She caught herself up abruptly. Her hand, which had strayed to his hair, now pressed against his chest in trembling restraint. He dragged his mouth away, expelling a shuddering sigh. For long moments, they gazed at each other. Antonia gave a nervous laugh.

"You were wrong, m'lord. I fear no one can match you in audacity. Whisking a lady from under her chaperon's eye for the sole purpose of stealing a kiss is brash in the extreme."

"A young lady who'd provoke such a retaliation must be said to have her share of daring," was his succinct reply.

"Retreating from your challenge would've been most cowardly of me."

"Mmm. And more so of me had I allowed you the upper hand." He plucked a rose from a nearby bush, freed it of thorns and proffered it with a tiny bow.

"You're saying you bested me in this scrimmage?" she murmured, lightly tracing a finger over the soft petals.

"You cried halt first," he reminded her.

"You play for high stakes, m'lord. How far must I be required to go before you'll concede defeat?"

"I'll fight to the end." Again his finger lifted her gaze to his. "I love the sweet taste of victory."

"I'll remember that, though I know not what you hope to gain."

She said the words flippantly, in the spirit of their verbal parrying, but inside, her heart hammered a warning. How easily the words "I love you" might have tripped off her tongue. It shook her to the core to question how they got there. More disconcerting was how willingly she could surrender heart and soul in the fire of his embrace. Michael was dangerous, and she'd best have a care lest she find herself once again in an extremely vulnerable position.

THE COACH HALTED before the Berkley residence. Antonia smoothed her hands down the length of her pink-dotted muslin and reached for her reticule, directing a tiny shrug to her maid. Polly smiled encouragement as the steps were let down for them to alight.

Cadby, the Berkley's butler, answered the knocker. A faint smile traced his lips as he ushered her inside. "Miss Berkley is in the music-room, Miss Marley," he intoned in a low voice. "I'll allow you to introduce yourself—master's orders." He gave a slight cough, and motioned to a bench set along the wall of the cool, scrubbed hallway. "Your maid is free to wait there, if it pleases you."

Antonia nodded in acquiescence, bade Polly wait, drew a deep breath and turned towards the music-room. Opening the door quietly, she slipped inside. Maria picked a lonely tune on the harp, her sad brown eyes lifted heavenward. Brown curls tumbled over her white muslin-clad shoulders and down her back. Rodney should see her like this, Antonia thought. "Maria?" she murmured.

Maria's fingers stilled. Her head snapped round, and her face grew cold and distant. "Why wasn't I informed you were here?"

"I suspect that's a question to ask your butler," Antonia prevaricated, disliking to implicate Maria's father in dealing behind her back.

"And so I shall!" Maria gained her feet, her shoulders squared, the light of battle in her eyes. "If you'd be pleased to remain here, Cadby will arrive directly to show you out."

Maria took a few steps towards the door, but Antonia, standing in front of it, had the advantage. She planted her feet and refused to budge, returning Maria's daggered look with a winning smile.

Maria folded her arms across her chest, one foot tapping in irritation. "Why are you here? Surely you took my hint the other day that the connexions between us are cut."

"Your *hint* spoke volumes, I assure you," Antonia returned, striving for calm. Her fingers moved to the ribbons of her suddenly constricting bonnet. Her chin tilted higher, and she pinned Maria with her direct regard. "I could scarce ignore your blatant disrespect of our friendship."

Maria returned look for look. "Did we have one?"

"I had imagined so. Search your heart."

Maria's gaze didn't falter, but her chin trembled and her eyes grew bright with tears. She wrung her hands and swung away to pace the tiled floor. "Oh, how am I to know who's dealing falsely with me? Yes, I suppose we were friends! Perhaps I even accused Rodney unjustly, but Morton Smythe—" She broke off, her shoulders slumping with obvious dejection. Sinking onto a chair, she began to cry. "I keep telling myself I'll get over Rodney in time, but it doesn't seem to be happening!"

Antonia took the chair next to Maria and placed a comforting hand on her arm. "What about Morton Smythe?"

Maria retrieved a dainty handkerchief and dabbed at her eyes. Hiccuping, she stared mournfully at her hands. "Morton's been my friend this age. He's always been kind and caring. When he began courting you, I was delighted, thinking how perfect it would be if you made a match of it, for then I'd be close to the people I most cared about."

She sniffed woefully. "Seeing as how he was so much in your company, I could scarce disbelieve him when he came to me with words straight from your mouth." She pleated the handkerchief in agitation, but didn't look up. "He was most distressed with the sorry news, but as my friend, he couldn't sit by and allow me to be taken in all unawares."

"Might I know the words he brought to you 'straight from my mouth'?" Antonia asked patiently.

"He said you'd told him your entire family was anticipating our wedding, as it would repair your depleted fortunes," Maria murmured. "That you gave Rodney credit for making such a brilliant match, as you hadn't thought him so sensible." Maria looked up, her eyes accusing.

"You may not want my opinion, Maria, but that man is a cad! He's played us both falsely, and I could wring his neck." Antonia's breath hissed between her teeth. "Mr Smythe misconstrued my words. I find it intolerable that he'd twist my comments to the detriment of so much happiness."

She sighed, spreading her hands. "'Tis no secret our family isn't precisely well-fixed. It's recently been brought to our attention that we're even sadder set than we thought However, as I recall, 'twas one of the concerns Rodney took to your father when he applied for your hand. He was fearful of being denied on account of his lack of worldly provisions.

"When Mr. Smythe commented—and it was *his* comment—that Rodney must be pleased to be making such a financially brilliant match, I merely agreed it was well you had a few pennies, as Rodney certainly did not. I meant to imply it would make your life together much more comfortable. You can't know how tiresome it is to always make do. I don't deny I privately considered it fortunate you're an heiress. 'Twould allow Rodney to rejuvenate the estate and realize a more profitable return than we're receiving thus far."

She shrugged. "I hope I'm not being grasping, but rather practical. I've no way of knowing if Rodney had actually considered the benefits of your fortune. But as to the charge that our entire family is anticipating the match, I respond by saying no more than anyone else who desires to see a loved one happy. For myself, I was exceedingly glad Rodney had chosen so suitably, as he'd been known to run with some rather fast company. I was pleased to welcome you into the family, not for your money, but for yourself, because you are so exactly suited to him. I considered you two the perfect complement to each other."

"Why would Morton lie to me?" asked Maria sadly.

Compassionate for her friend's pain, Antonia answered in soft tones, "Mayhap he's the fortune-hunter?"

Maria bit her lip, and a single tear splashed onto her hand. She nodded. "It must be as you say. I'm sorry, Antonia. I've grossly mismanaged this entire affair. I should've spoken with you before ever I attacked Rodney." She wrung the unfortunate handkerchief through her hands. "I've made the greatest muddle! Poor Rodney! He'll never speak to me again, and I do love him so!"

She burst into tears again. "I've been perfectly miserable. It near broke my heart to think he only wanted my money. How could I have believed Morton over him? Morton!" she spat with distaste. "I should've seen through him from the start. But I was so hurt thinking Rodney would trifle with my affections. Now what am I to do?"

Antonia eyed her with sympathy, at a loss as to how to console her. "Maria, you can but try again. I won't deny Rodney's furious—he feels you've cast a dreadful slur on his integrity. An apology might be the first step in smoothing the path between you."

"Yes, of course I shall apologize," said Maria, dabbing at her eyes with the handkerchief. "And I shall wring Morton Smythe's lying neck."

"As to that..." Antonia launched into the plans already being laid for the rascal. "The most prudent action might be to say nothing until Rodney has a go at him," she cautioned. "I shouldn't like to see him cheated of his satisfaction."

"Neither should I," Maria agreed, revealing the ghost of a smile. "I'll be delighted when Morton receives his comeuppance. Papa has told me forever that he's a scoundrel, but I couldn't accept it. Now that I've spoken with you, so many things have fallen into place. I can't like treating him graciously, but I shall until after Rodney has had his match. 'Tis the least I can do to make amends."

"You could quarrel with Morton on some completely irrelevant matter," Antonia suggested. "Promise you'll forgive him soon, and thus, keep him dangling. You might find a measure of satisfaction in that."

A full smile wreathed Maria's face. "A capital notion! I'll draw up plans immediately." A tiny giggle bubbled free, and she leaned forward to capture Antonia in a warm embrace. "I apologize for my rudeness. Thank you for coming. I feel much more the thing."

"I'm thankful you listened, Maria," Antonia returned, drawing away to gaze at her in earnest. "I hope you know we'd never hurt you intentionally."

Maria nodded. "You'll put in a good word for me?"

"I'll do more than that. Come to tea. Between the two of us, we might hit on a scheme to bring Rodney round."

Maria beamed. "Thank you."

CHAPTER TEN

UPON HER RETURN HOME, Antonia learned that Lord Wilson awaited her company in the drawing-room. The pleasure she'd gained from her encounter with Maria vanished. She grimaced, turning reluctant steps towards the unescapable.

Garbed in turquoise and canary yellow, Lord Wilson's fat frame dominated the room. Antonia greeted him in polite tones, adjuring him not to rise on her account.

"So gracious, my dear," he assured her, forsaking his attempt to do just that. Settling back onto his chair, he beamed at her with proprietorial eyes. "Your aunt and I were discussing you. Told her I bet she never thought I'd be dangling after her pretty little niece. Heh, heh."

"I assured him that was quite so," Matilda intervened, casting her niece a wicked glance. "Have some tea, Antonia, do." Antonia received the proffered cup with thanks, and chose a chair close to her aunt.

"Quite frankly, though," Lord Wilson continued seriously, "young Alton concerns me. Take my advice, Miss Marley, and don't let these young swains sweep you off your feet. They're unstable, the lot of them."

"Indeed," Antonia murmured, throwing her aunt a disbelieving glance over the rim of her cup.

He gave a firm nod. "You'd be wise to see 'em for what they are, m'dear. They tinker with your affections.... I know, heh, heh. Used to be a young man once myself.

"Now I'm more worldly-wise, and yes, quite honourable. That can be proven in that I've already taken an offer to your papa. Place these young gallants aside of me—" he smiled smugly, flicking a speck of lint from his coat "—and they can't afford to be serious in their intentions. So be wise, m'dear, and know which side your bread is buttered on. Don't run from the mature hand you so need into those of a callow youth. I can offer you so much more." A large, self-satisfied smile split his face. "You will drive with me in the Park tomorrow?"

Antonia, who'd stared at him in speechless amazement throughout his dialogue, snapped to attention. "I've a previous engagement," she improvised, scarcely heeding when Michael and Rodney joined them. "A young swain," she claimed rather tartly, "who no doubt can't afford to be honourable in his intentions."

Lord Wilson spluttered and directed a malevolent look upon Michael. "My Lord Alton," he proclaimed, "I'll thank you to quit encroaching upon my territory."

Michael drew himself to his full height and peered down his nose in the most dignified manner. "I'm sure I've never poached upon your land before, m'lord. Besides, 'tis not I who claims Miss Marley's time on the morrow."

"Oh, that yellow-haired rascal, is it? Now there's a bounder, if every I saw one!"

"Delbert!" Matilda hastily intervened, casting her niece a warning glance. "Do tell us how your daughters go on!" It was more a command than a request.

"Eh?" he asked, instinctively recoiling from the dish of bon-bons thrust in his face. Recognizing the offering, he relaxed and selected a few, popping one into his mouth. "Oh, quite well, quite well. Harriet, the eldest, is recuperating from her third. Finally gave her husband a strong son, and well past time, I'd say. I'd almost despaired she wasn't woman enough. Too bad the little whipper-snapper doesn't bear my name. Mean to rectify that matter soon, though." His killing glare ran Michael through.

Michael raised his brows in answer.

"They both managed the birth in good health?" Matilda rushed to ask, again thrusting the bowl of sweets at him.

"Oh yes, quite," he replied, choosing another, though he still held two in his hand. "And, er, how is your health, Miss Marley?"

"Oh, quite well, quite well," she returned, unable to deny the urge to mimic him. It was her turn to receive a killing look, this one from her aunt.

Lord Wilson didn't notice she was making game of him and he nodded with approval. "Glad to hear it, m'dear. Heard the rumour you were out of sorts not very long ago. Perhaps you shouldn't gallivant about with such regularity. One round of gaiety after another can only be detrimental to the health."

"No doubt," she agreed, her tone docile, though her foot was set to tapping.

"Yes, yes," said Lord Wilson. "Guess I'd best be taking my leave before you make me fat with those bon-bons, Matilda. Heh, heh." He struggled to his feet, patting his bulging middle. "No need to show me out. Don't believe in this standing on ceremony nonsense. Miss Marley," he bowed over her hand, "I trust you'll remember my words of wisdom." Straightening, he nodded to the room in general. "Good day to you all."

He quit their company amidst a chorus of hearty sighs.

"I declare!" exclaimed Matilda. "I cannot know what your father is about, encouraging that man. That was certainly the most onerous tea I've ever taken. I hope I needn't repeat the experience soon."

"He's a *grandfather,*" Antonia announced in accents of loathing. "I never thought Papa capable of such villainy! And I shall write and tell him so!"

Michael put a hand to the curtains drawing them back to peer out the window. Gads. Would his conscience never stop plaguing him? He wanted to confess the lot, but he didn't. He clamped his jaw shut and squared his shoulders.

"Don't be hasty," Matilda cautioned. "We wouldn't want him coming to London to make you be civil to the man. I don't want him interfering with our plans, and I can tell you, I *won't* welcome a repeat of today's fiasco. And as to Wilson being a grandfather, his daughters married quite young, I believe."

"He's still old enough to be my father," Antonia stated, her fine brows fixed in a black frown.

"So he is, but I shouldn't worry your head about it," her aunt replied. "I've already promised I won't stand by and watch you marry him."

Michael wanted to turn about and shout, "Marry me, and have done with this coil!" But he didn't. He couldn't afford to. Not yet.

"Now," Matilda continued, "we have a week until the duchess's ball—I must go shopping. I have just the thing in mind...." She trailed out of the room, her face a mask of concentration.

"Oh, the ball," Antonia groaned. "I don't suppose I can hope he won't be there. I vow I shall hate it if I have to dance with him."

"We can fix that quite easily," Rodney claimed. "Just have your dance card filled before ever we arrive."

"Am I to go about soliciting dances in the week?" she asked, humour lighting her eyes.

"I'll claim two right now," Michael intoned. "A waltz and a supper dance." A smile quirked his lips. "If, that is, you'd so honour me?"

He looked so endearingly uncertain, as if he weren't sure she would. Small wonder though, since she'd warily kept him at arm's length since their stroll through the garden. Rodney intervened before she could form a warm reply.

"Of course she will," he asserted. "I must say, you two are going about this thing all wrong. Gads, Antonia, how's Society ever to know you favour Michael when one day you're driving with him, and the next with Harvey? With Lord Wilson forever tagging behind, 'tis not likely you'll escape attention. Next we know, they'll be drawing up bets at White's, speculating on who will win your hand."

"They're already drawing up bets at White's," Michael softly informed them. "Oh, a handful of fribbles, nothing serious yet."

"How dare they?" Antonia cried. "And who, m'lord, are they wagering will triumph?"

He lifted one shoulder in a half shrug. "Some say none of us will; you've eluded many beaux ere now. Some are betting on the dark horse—Lord Wilson, that is. A couple say myself, but the majority favour Harvey—young, handsome, with a good degree of wealth. Some argue the title will out; most concede the fortune will."

He shook his head, casting her an apologetic glance. "They're a bunch of mindless dolts, Antonia, with nothing better to do than make ridiculous wagers. I shouldn't concern myself with them. I'm sorry I said anything, for I didn't mean to cause you upset."

"No, no," she said, spreading her hands. "'Tis well I know what they're saying. Rodney's right, I haven't taken this matter seriously enough." Which was a lie. She was taking it too seriously—precisely why she needed to put distance between herself and Michael by being with Alex. She frowned. "However, I can't like discouraging Alex out of hand. I'll need a husband someday, and he is a charming companion."

She peeked from under her lashes and caught Michael's reaction—a quick scowl—before he bent his head and studied his nails. "You don't like him, do you, Michael?"

"Like whom?" he returned, lifting his head, his expression enigmatic.

"Alex Harvey."

A tight smile formed on his lips. "Don't be silly. He's my cousin."

"Well, I don't like him above half," Rodney declared. "Were I you, Antonia, I'd give him the roundabout. It won't do, keeping him on a leading string whilst we attend to matters of greater import. And it's most important you and Michael appear to be falling in love.

"The duchess's ball will give you the perfect opportunity to exercise your acting talents. You must especially keep your heads together over supper. Michael, find a secluded table, and *flirt!* Antonia, smile and laugh—some warm glances wouldn't come amiss. Above all, you must appear besotted."

Antonia and Michael exchanged glances, grinning widely. "Quite an authority on the subject, is he not?" Michael chuckled. "Shall we procure him a podium?"

"Well, dash it all," Rodney grumbled, "you can't discuss the weather, or compare gowns all evening. Seems to me you two are doing a wary dance round each other. If you're going to come off halfway convincing, you'll have to flirt."

"And so we shall," was Michael's smooth promise. Bless Rodney's intervening heart. Every moment he spent with Antonia was one moment less she could spend with Alex

Harvey. "I'm not a complete dolt in the art of making love. I assure you, heads shall be together in speculation ere the night is over."

"I never meant to imply that you were a dolt," Rodney disclaimed, scowling at his sister's burst of laughter.

"Shall I keep a list to see just how well he performs?" she asked, mischief lighting her eyes.

"Ah, the lady is forever issuing challenges," Michael murmured, his eyes radiating a wicked gleam. "She should know better by now."

Antonia sobered, though humour still danced in her eyes. "And so I should," she conceded. "You're a hard man to best."

"'Tis my competitive nature. I try never to let anyone get the better of me. Unless it's my decision to allow it." Laughter sparkled in the dark depths of his own eyes.

"You're that sure of yourself?" she queried with a smile.

His shrug was nonchalant, but he spoke in serious tones. "If a man lacks confidence, he could well lose the battle before e'er it's begun."

"Good word, Michael," said Rodney. He gave a slight frown. "You don't suppose Smythe could best me, do you?"

"Not a chance of it," Michael replied with conviction.

"Didn't think so," Rodney agreed. "Especially after you show me those moves you promised. By the by, Annie, I believe you spoke with our fine lady in her mansion today?"

Antonia wasn't fooled by his studied indifference. Though she'd like to tease him, she thought better of it, and launched into an account of her visit with Maria. She portrayed that lady in the light of a despairing heroine, mentioning her sadness, her tears, her contriteness, and above all, her indignation against Mr. Smythe.

Rodney remained unmoved, exerting himself only to ask if Maria would keep mum about their plans regarding Smythe, as if he suspected her to deal treacherously. Antonia quickly disabused him of this notion.

"Maria thinks it a famous idea. She assured me she'd give no hint of her knowledge until you've had a chance to wreak your vengeance. She hoped it might serve in some small way to make repayment for her accusing you unjustly."

Rodney grunted. "Noble of her, I'm sure," was his cold comment.

"Rodney! People aren't perfect. They make mistakes."

"She chose Smythe's word over mine," Rodney returned without softening. "Come, Michael, show me those moves."

Antonia realized it was useless to argue further. The men stripped off their jackets and cleared a space on the floor. Propriety dictated she remove herself from their presence, but she wasn't prepared to concede, deciding it was far more entertaining to watch Michael's back muscles ripple beneath his white cambric shirt. He pushed up his sleeves, displaying strong, sun-bronzed forearms. His handsome thighs stretched against his buff-coloured breeches. Antonia curled into a comfortable ball, her eyes glowing with admiration for this remarkable sight.

"TANNER," MICHAEL SAID, rising to meet his right-hand man. "Have you anything to report?"

"Nothing yet, guv. Mr. Harvey's been good as gold. He's a mean 'un, though. He sure does yell at those servants of his. If you'll forgive my saying so, Miss Antonia don't want nothin' to do with him."

Unfortunately, it sounded to Michael as if she did. However could he woo her, when she had eyes for that rapscallion? He resumed his chair, and glanced again at Tanner, who rocked from one foot to the other in an uncomfortable silence. "You have someone following him at all hours?"

"Yes, guv. I myself take duty when somethin' big is happenin', like them goin' to and from the Park, and whatnot."

Michael nodded. "The Duchess of Leavenworth's ball is soon. I'd like you to take that night as well, just in case."

"Yes, sir."

"Very well. Keep a close eye on him. That's all, Tanner."

"Good day to you, m'lord."

"Good day."

The study door closed behind Tanner, and Michael stared at it. Time was running short. Antonia, as was her wont, was meddling in Rodney and Maria's affair, and if she had her way, as she usually did, she'd have the two cozying up in no time. Lord Wilson was sure to tire of her lack of affection, too. And here she was, spouting some ridiculous faradiddle about Harvey being charming! Calling him by his given name, too. What was Michael to do with her? She'd been avoiding him since that night in Matilda's garden.

He rested his chin on his twined fingers. Hadn't she liked his kiss? If not, then why her delicious response? His eyes closed at the memory, and he caught his breath. So soft, so warm, so *feminine*. Gads, the woman was creeping under his skin! He wanted to kiss her again and again. 'Twas one possibility he hadn't considered. He'd watched her, wondering how, wills and plots aside, he'd feel about taking her to wife. The notion sounded demmed pleasing.

He shook his head. Best to keep focused on Uncle George's will, and use his good sense to figure how Miss Antonia Marley might be made his bride.

CHAPTER ELEVEN

DESPITE RODNEY'S ADVICE, Antonia found she couldn't like dismissing Alex out of hand. Always there loomed an end to this charade, and her fate once the "engagement" was broken. Alex was most attentive in his pursuit, and she wondered if she might not expect an offer from him soon. She quailed at the thought of bringing him pain, but wasn't sure she could pledge herself to him in all faithfulness. Drat Michael's handsome eyes! She knew well the fine line she toed, all the while protecting herself from what she dared not feel.

She drove with Alex the following day. Though enjoying his company, she couldn't help comparing the two cousins. Michael's easy charm and subtle humour had always delighted her, whereas finding rapport with Alex's stinging wit was difficult.

He'd dubbed Lord Wilson "the pudgy parrot," and grumbled when he trailed them yet again. Antonia couldn't like the man herself, but found the references rather mean. Michael would've taken it in stride, using his fertile brain to devise some method of shaking the fellow. They'd laugh together after they'd succeeded in thwarting him once again.

"Perhaps Rodney and Sir Lawrence would be pleased to detain him for us," she suggested, indicating the two men with a nod of her head.

"'Tis worth a try," Alex agreed, pulling up beside them.

Sir Lawrence laughed before she could speak. His gaze swivelled to Lord Wilson, and he clucked with good-humour. "That man possesses the most singular taste in fashion. I must compliment him immediately on his, er...striking choice of colours. That orange and green," he said, smacking his lips, "is ever so eye-catching! Quite reminds me of a jester I once saw." His ready smile lit his face. "Before I leave you, Miss Marley, might I beg you to save three dances for my cousins and I at the duchess's ball?"

Antonia laughed at the appealing lift of his brows, her eyes darting to Rodney, whose lips formed a complacent smile. "I'd be pleased to," she answered Sir Lawrence. "Have you any preference to which ones?"

"A quadrille for myself. My cousins aren't here to choose, so they'll take what they can get." Lawrie tipped his hat. "Good day, Miss Marley. I look forward to seeing you then." He executed a slight bow towards Alex, then turned his mount to accost Lord Wilson. Rodney echoed his actions.

"Already giving away your dances, Antonia?" Alex queried, urging his team into motion. "Might I solicit your supper dance and a waltz?"

"My supper dance is already secured, but you shall certainly have a waltz," she promised, then hurried on lest he should ask who she had promised to dine with. "'Tis my intention to have my card filled, with fictitious names if I must, before e'er I arrive. I haven't any desire to dance with Lord Wilson."

"Ah, and your brother's doing much of your footwork, eh?"

"It would seem so." She caught sight of Michael, speaking with Lady Davenport and her beautiful daughter. Exceedingly handsome in doeskin breeches and a bottle-green coat, he sat his black with graceful ease. She hated the smile

Lucy wore for him. He glanced up, smiled at seeing her, and doffed his hat. Antonia smiled in return, raising her hand in a tiny salute.

The phaeton jerked forward at a faster pace, throwing her slightly off balance. Surprised, she glanced at Alex, noting the quick scowl darkening his features. She might have imagined it though, for a moment later, his lips lifted in an apologetic smile. His next words assured her she'd misinterpreted his frown.

"Sorry. I'm afraid my team is a bit restive. I normally have Carlisle take the edge off their high spirits, but he hadn't the chance today. Tell me you'll drive with me tomorrow. I promise to give you a better showing."

Remembering Rodney's strictures, she hastened to say, "I can't. I'm sorry, but I shall have the headache."

He stared at her quizzically. "You're able to predict those things?"

She uttered an unsteady laugh, feeling the greatest dolt, but was quick to improvise. "I can when I know Lord Wilson is coming to tea. 'Twould make my falsehood remarkable were I to claim such illness, and be caught out driving."

He laughed. "And will you be ill the rest of the week, as well?"

"That depends upon how assiduous his attentions become. I mean to make myself as fatiguing as possible. We endured the most trying of teas with him yesterday. I don't care to repeat the experience."

"Can't your aunt simply refuse him admittance?"

"What good would it do? Surely you've guessed by now that the man is unshakable?"

"I'd be rather a slowtop if I hadn't," he conceded with a chuckle. "And speaking of which, I should probably step up the pace lest he catch us again."

He dropped her at her aunt's a short while later, promising to call within the week.

"MR. SMYTHE IS falling over himself trying to please me," Maria confided to Antonia as they sipped tea and munched macaroons in Antonia's cozy sitting-room. "I have him going in so many directions, I daresay he'll be dizzy soon." Her eyes danced wickedly.

"He's fair screaming with vexation, though he hasn't uttered a word against me. I tell him my nerves are all about and that he's the best of good friends for bearing with me, then I snap at him for bringing me a bon-bon of the wrong colour. His perfidy sickens me, but—" she smiled "—exacting my revenge is vastly entertaining."

"He's no notion you're onto him?" Antonia asked, laughing with her. How well Maria looked today, the bloom returned to her cheeks and a lively light in her eyes. Her dusky curls framed her pretty face, enhancing those wide, dark eyes. Her blue muslin gown became her exceedingly.

"Not a bit of it. Papa's been a complete hand. I related the whole story, and he's been wonderfully supportive. He told me all kinds of little tricks I could use to get Morton's dander up. It's ever so fun plotting with him. He's quite pleased you had the backbone to approach me, and I'm to convey his thanks." She studied Antonia. "I can expect anything of Papa. Did he speak with you behind my back?"

A tinkle of laughter escaped Antonia. "I hope you don't take it amiss?"

"Not at all. I'm glad he did. After you left the other day, I wondered how it was you'd known Morton was spreading tales—how you knew enough, in fact, that Rodney was already setting about drawing up battle plans...."

Antonia clapped a hand over her mouth, her eyes shimmering. "I thought I'd been so crafty! What a peagoose I am. Did you ask your father about it?"

Maria laughed. "No, I couldn't like making him aware I was onto his scheming. He likes me to think he never questions my ability to make sound decisions."

"'Tis too funny, Maria. I can scarce credit I so unwittingly let the cat out of the bag. I do hope our meddling hasn't angered you."

"Do I appear angry? Indeed, I'm most grateful—"

The door was suddenly opened to admit Rodney. Maria's cup slid from her nerveless fingers, clattering loudly onto its saucer. Rodney stilled, his attention centred wholly upon the dainty lady in blue muslin. Antonia was pleased to watch their reactions. Maria's eyes grew wider, her lips parting slightly. Rodney stood at rigid attention, only his eyes expressing emotion as they drank in the sight of her.

The moment lasted but an instant. Rodney cleared his throat. "Sorry, Antonia, I didn't realize you have company." He executed a small, stiff bow in Maria's direction. "Miss Berkley."

Maria paled at the formality, then gathered her dignity. Eyes flashing, she tilted her head. "Mr. Marley."

Antonia moved into action. "Rodney, 'tis so fortunate you arrived. Maria and I have a notion to sample Cook's apple tarts, but someone neglected to include them on the tray. I do dislike leaving Maria alone to fetch James to bring some.... Would you keep her company for a few minutes whilst I seek him out?"

She gave him no time to decline, though his expression spoke volumes. She threw him a disarming smile before sailing out the door. Maria would need but a minute to effect her apology. Rodney, she suspected, was in no mood for

Here are your BIG WIN Game Tickets, worth from $10.00 to $1,000,000.00 each. Scratch off the PINK METALLIC STRIP on each of your Sweepstakes tickets to see what you could win and mail your entry right away. (SEE OFFICIAL RULES IN BACK OF BOOK FOR DETAILS!)

This could be your lucky day—GOOD LUCK!

FOLD AND DETACH ALONG THIS DOTTED LINE—RETURN ALL GAME TICKETS INTACT.

1 Scratch PINK METALLIC STRIP to reveal potential value of this ticket if it is a winning ticket. Return all game tickets intact.

5B 559241

2 THE BIG WIN — LUCKY NUMBER

Scratch PINK METALLIC STRIP to reveal potential value of this ticket if it is a winning ticket. Return all game tickets intact.

7W 546835

3 Scratch PINK METALLIC STRIP to reveal potential value of this ticket if it is a winning ticket. Return all game tickets intact.

2F 555128

4 THE BIG WIN — LUCKY NUMBER

Scratch PINK METALLIC STRIP to reveal potential value of this ticket if it is a winning ticket. Return all game tickets intact.

6I 570219

5 We're giving away brand new books to selected individuals. Scratch PINK METALLIC STRIP for number of free books you will receive.

130107-742

6 FREE GIFT — AUTHORIZATION CODE

We have an outstanding added gift for you if you are accepting our free books. Scratch PINK METALLIC STRIP to reveal gift.

130107-742

YES! Enter my Lucky Numbers in THE BIG WIN Sweepstakes, and when winners are selected, tell me if I've won any prize. If PINK METALLIC STRIP is scratched off on ticket #5, I will also receive one or more FREE Harlequin Regency Romance™ novels along with the FREE GIFT on ticket #6, as explained on the opposite page.

248 CIH ADN4 (U-H-RG-01/92)

NAME ______________________________

ADDRESS ______________________ APT. ________

CITY ______________ STATE ________ ZIP ________

Offer limited to one per household and not valid to current Harlequin Regency Romance subscribers.

a gracious acceptance. She hastened down the stairs, seeking James with impatience.

Her skirts rustling, she swished past the drawing-room door, halting in dismay when her aunt called her name. "Not now, Aunt Mattie," she moaned, quickly retracing her steps. "I'm in the greatest of rushes. Rodney and Maria are closeted in my sitting-room, and I mustn't be but a moment." She checked, espying her aunt wasn't alone. "Oh, hello, Michael."

He barely managed a greeting.

"Alone in your sitting-room?" Matilda exclaimed. "Antonia, that's highly improper."

"Which is why I'm rushing. It'll take Maria but a moment to speak her piece, and what with Rodney being in such a pig-headed mode, I doubt they'll have much conversation after that. But I must find James to bring some apple tarts—'twas my excuse for leaving them alone." She spied the tea-tray near her aunt. "Oh, you have some. Do you mind if I pilfer a couple?" Without waiting for an answer, she procured a plate and helped herself.

Don't fail me now, Rodney, Michael thought. *Don't make up with her yet.* Blast Antonia—and she looked happy as a lark. But then, she imagined her problems would be solved by their reunion.

"Meddlesome chit," chastised her aunt. Antonia smiled brightly in agreement, and Matilda sent her a disapproving frown. "I don't suppose it has occurred to you to let them work it out on their own, without your interference?"

"Why, no," Antonia responded, pausing in reflection. "However can they work it out if they haven't the opportunity to do so? Besides, Rodney won't come to face it unless he's forced to."

"Amazing how alike you two are in that respect," murmured Matilda. "One only hopes it doesn't take him three years to come about."

Antonia's gaze flew to Michael. He confronted her with an enigmatic stare. "Indeed," she murmured. "But I don't have three years for Rodney to come round." She turned on her heel, hastening from the room.

"Be sure to tell Rodney that Michael awaits," Matilda called after her.

Antonia paused outside the sitting-room door. Was it good or bad that no sound came from within? She pushed the door open, a dazzling smile affixed on her face. Rodney stood stiffly by the window; Maria sat primly, her hands folded in her lap. The atmosphere was decidedly strained.

"Here we are," Antonia sang, depositing her offering on the tea-table. "Rodney, thank you for keeping my guest company. I appreciate your kindness. Michael awaits you below."

Rodney nodded in acknowledgement, piercing her with a knowing look as he passed by. At the door, he turned and gave a slight bow. "Good day, Miss Berkley."

Maria gave a single nod. "Mr. Marley."

"Oh, dear," Antonia murmured. "It didn't go so well, I think."

Maria chuckled, a soft, nervous sound. "I can't pretend it was comfortable, but I'm glad of the opportunity to redeem myself. It gave me the chance to gauge Rodney's position—his arctic manner makes me believe he won't be easily won." She straightened her shoulders. "But I shan't give up. I love him, and love is worth fighting for."

Antonia nodded, her brow creased in a frown. She herself didn't have the courage to love, much less fight for it.

"Maria, there's something you must know about our financial position. I tell you this in confidence, only so you won't have cause to take umbrage again. We are indeed in the basket, so much so, in fact—"

"Rodney told me about Lord Wilson and your need to find a parti. I'm sorry, Antonia, this entire muddle is my fault. 'Tis my wicked temper." Antonia made an effort to demure, but Maria waved it away. "No, it is. I should've realized I'd love Rodney even if he were a fortune-hunter." She giggled. "I fear he told me the news to provoke a negative reaction, but he didn't succeed." In earnest again, she rested her hand on Antonia's arm. "I wish you the best. Lord Wilson was pointed out to me yesterday.... Such a fate would be unbearable. If only Rodney would come about—I would marry him tomorrow if it would save you!"

"Thank you, Maria," Antonia said with a grateful smile. "But you mustn't concern yourself for me. I'll set sail for America before I marry him."

"I shouldn't think you'll have to. I've seen Alex Harvey and Lord Alton squiring you about the Park. I was most surprised to see you and Lord Alton laughing together." Her eyes twinkled. "You have two of London's most eligible bachelors at your fingertips, and I've never considered you a slowtop."

The problem was, thought Antonia, if she got a chance to choose, which of them would she have? The one she knew could never break her heart, or the one who already had?

CHAPTER TWELVE

Clad in undergarments, Antonia perched before her vanity, tapping an impatient foot whilst Polly laboriously swept her hair into an elaborate coiffure. "Shouldn't I get into my gown first?" she asked for the third time. "The blue satin wreaks vengeance on the hair."

Polly sighed aloud and reiterated in patient tones, "Your aunt said I was to have you bathed, smelling pretty, and your hair done. That's all. She's going to choose your gown; you've worn that blue satin thrice already. She's certain she'll swoon if she sees you in't again." She looked up from her work. "I think she's going to give you loan of her diamonds. I heard her muttering about diamonds, anyway."

"But I haven't anything to wear with diamonds," Antonia said in despair, "and the blue satin is my finest gown."

Polly shrugged and pinned the last curl into place. She dipped her fingers in a bowl of sugar water and patted at a few loose hairs. Surveying her handiwork, she beamed when Antonia exclaimed, "Why, Polly, this is the prettiest arrangement you've ever concocted."

"'Tis lovely, indeed," agreed Matilda. She bustled into the room, a vision of amethyst silk, with matching stones at her ears and neck.

"Aunt," laughed Antonia, "I must protest your abuse of my blue satin. I know I've worn it too much for good taste, but I thought perhaps a sash and a white rose..."

Matilda shook her head firmly, crossing the room. "It amazes me, Niece, how seldom you look in your wardrobe. I'm certain I saw just the thing in here not an hour hence. Ah, yes..." She pulled forth a graceful creation of shimmery silver gauze, holding it up for inspection.

Polly gasped and Antonia laughed with delight. "Oh, Aunt Mattie, 'tis simply gorgeous," she breathed, throwing her arms round that lady's neck in a fierce hug.

Matilda chuckled, easing her away. "Careful, don't crush the material. Polly, help her into it. I'm all atwitter to see if it fits aright."

"Oh, yes, Polly, do hurry," Antonia begged. Polly moved with reverent care, but no sooner did the fine material swirl about her ankles than Antonia demanded to look in the glass.

"Not so hasty, child," her aunt admonished, peeking again into the wardrobe. "Seems I saw a pair of slippers, too.... There they are. Polly, I daresay if you look in her jewellery box, you'll find a delightful hair ornament. Antonia, put these on."

Antonia stared, bemused at the fine offerings. She accepted the slippers thrust at her, marvelling at their perfect match to her gown. She slipped them on and allowed Polly to secure the silver filigreed ornament in her hair.

"And now the diamonds." Matilda produced a box from the bureau. The cool weight of the gems encircled her throat, and Antonia sighed her delight. She twisted her head, and the sparkling ear-rings brushed against her neck. Matilda stood back, surveying her with a critical eye. She snapped her fingers. "Dear me," she said, rummaging through the bureau again. "Mustn't forget these...or this." She drew forth a pair of white gloves adorned with silver braiding and a matching reticule.

"Aunt, how can I thank you?" Antonia cried. "I vow I'll be the finest lady at the ball!" She carefully fitted the elbow-length gloves, then slipped the reticule string round her wrist. Gazing imploringly at her aunt, she asked, "Now may I look in the mirror?"

"I should feel cruel if I didn't let you," laughed Matilda.

"Oh," breathed Antonia, twirling before the glass, marvelling that the simple Grecian cut fit her slender figure to perfection. The brilliant diamonds sparkled against her creamy skin, the hair ornament glistened against her dark curls. "Oh," she breathed again. "I look—"

"Beautiful?" queried her aunt. "Stunning, enchanting, ethereal? Yes, my dear, all of those." Matilda's smile bespoke her utter satisfaction.

Antonia caught her gaze in the glass. "Aunt, all this finery...do you have ulterior motives?"

Matilda smiled, much like a cat in the cream. "Of course, my dear. You've a husband to catch, remember? I vow m'lord Alton shall be captivated this night! And if he's not, I'll think him the veriest chucklehead. Now come, he and Rodney await below."

Antonia's nervous hand fluttered to her bosom. "He's to escort us?"

"Yes, did I fail to mention that?"

"Mmm." Antonia paused again before the mirror, trying to accustom herself to her regal appearance. "I feel so grand."

"You do look a picture, miss, and that's a fact," Polly agreed. "Your fine earl don't stand a chance, he don't."

"I hope you're right," she whispered.

"Come, Antonia."

"Yes, Aunt." Head high, she left the sanctuary of her chamber, descending the stairs with a floating grace. She felt like a fairy princess, though her heart palpitated with nervous anticipation. What would Michael think?

Michael stood at the sideboard, pouring a drink. Rodney's low whistle brought his head round and the decanter clanked back to the sideboard. He approached her, approval stamped on his face.

A warm glow suffused Antonia as he performed an elegant leg over her hand. He himself appeared to devastating advantage in his black evening clothes, his snowy white shirt in handsome contrast. Diamonds gleamed on his cuffs, and one sparkled from his starched cravat.

"Your beauty defies words," he murmured, his tones husky. His eyes lifted in a slow journey from the low-cut bodice of her gown to her face. "Were I poetic, I'd claim you outshine the stars."

"Thank you, Michael," she said demurely, her lashes sweeping down in sudden shyness.

"Fit to slay the staunchest hearts," Rodney added, appraising her from head to toe while proffering a drink.

"Thank you, Brother," Recovering her composure, Antonia smiled and received the glass. "I hope that doesn't mean there'll be a shortage of dance partners, though."

Michael guided her to a chair whilst Matilda looked on in satisfied approval. He selected a chair opposite her, and kept her in his fixed regard. Was it possible she stood a chance of gaining his approbation?

But no, their game had begun in earnest, and she adjured her heart to have a care. She was embarking on one of the greatest challenges she'd met thus far—that of remaining emotionally aloof whilst playing lovers with a man she dared not love again. By the time she curtsied to the Duchess of Leavenworth, she realized she was woefully unprepared for the onslaught of Michael's charm.

Acutely conscious of his guiding hand at the small of her back, Antonia wended her way through the crush of the ballroom. Only the smallest portion of her attention was given to following her aunt; the majority focused upon the warmth of Michael's touch. With lowered lashes, she savoured the contact, plowing blindly into Matilda's back when her aunt halted in front of her.

Antonia was caught off balance, but Michael's hands, closing firmly about her waist, instantly steadied her. He held her captive against him for heart-stopping moments, and it took effort to gain her breath, so unsettling was the contact. Matilda sent a dark glance over her shoulder, and Antonia compressed her lips against a giggle, contriving an apologetic visage. Michael chuckled softly in her ear, squeezing her waist before removing his hands. A flush of pleasure warmed Antonia's cheeks.

Antonia's dance card was filled by the time they found places to sit. Provident, she decided, especially when Matilda nudged her, nodding towards Lord Wilson. He saw them at that precise moment, and made a beeline in their direction. His evening attire consisted of maroon velvet breeches and coat. Though not lacking in taste, its effect was spoiled by a bright yellow waistcoat spilling with fobs and watches.

"A dance, Miss Marley," he huffed when he reached her, flicking out an imperious hand for her card.

Antonia glanced at her card and gave a sorrowful shake of her head. "I'm sorry, Lord Wilson, my card it quite filled."

"Filled? Preposterous. The music hasn't even begun." Much to her annoyance, he grasped her wrist, peering nearsightedly at the card. He grunted, dropped her arm and assumed a militant stance. "Miss Marley, I assure you, your continued avoidance of me goes quite against the grain.

Should you persist in this attitude, I shan't be held accountable for the withdrawal of my offer."

"Stubble it, Delbert," Matilda snapped, rapping him soundly on the hand with her fan.

He blustered, puffed out his chest, turned on his high heels and marched away. Antonia and Matilda exchanged glances of mild disbelief.

Michael pulled a chair next to Antonia's. "You've made progress," he congratulated her. "Lord Wilson's finally realized you're taking pains to stay out of his way. I'm glad he didn't notice me lest he challenge me to a duel."

Antonia laughed, nodding in agreement. "We seem to have lost Rodney," she observed.

"He's over there, talking with Maria." Michael indicated the couple with a nod of his head. Antonia craned her neck, following his direction.

"Oh, famous," she murmured. "Look, he's signing her card. I'm so pleased." The shy smile on Maria's face said she was, too. "There comes Morton Smythe." Michael's brows lifted with interest, and together they followed the progress of the scene. "I hope Rodney behaves."

Rodney turned to face his adversary, sweeping the man a disparaging glance and a cursory nod. Mr. Smythe bowed before Maria and her hand fluttered nervously. Antonia sighed with relief.

Michael watched in doomed silence. Lord Wilson spouting off to Antonia; Rodney soliciting a dance with Maria. He'd best make this night's work worthwhile. His time grew shorter with every minute.

The music began, and Michael departed to claim his first partner. Antonia thought it a shame they were allowed only two dances. Albert Halverson, her partner, was as boyishly handsome as Lawrie, and quite as charming, though he lacked his cousin's Town polish. Antonia, experiencing the unique sensation of intimidating a man, exerted herself to put him at ease. This accomplished, their dance passed in friendly harmony.

A succession of dances followed. Antonia was grateful to be returned to her aunt when the musicians took their break. She sank down beside her, fanning herself with vigour. Michael appeared with a glass of punch, which she accepted with thanks. She found it laced with some unidentified alcoholic beverage, and very tasty.

Matilda leaned towards her. "You're creating quite a stir, Niece," she commented in an undertone. "I've received any number of compliments on you already."

"Lady Hawthorne... haloo, haloo?" shrilled an irritatingly strident voice.

"Isobel," Matilda said with a grimace. A second later, her eyes lit in a magical transformation of expression. "Why, Isobel!" she exclaimed. "How pleasant to see you. Come, have a seat and chat." She patted the chair beside her, which Mrs. Lowry unhesitatingly availed herself of.

Antonia peered past Matilda and smiled a greeting. Glancing back to her aunt, she grinned slowly as comprehension dawned. "Capital," she whispered, provoking a raised brow from Michael. Isobel was perfect for Lord Wilson. Young, being some years above or below thirty, she was healthy, forward, and singularly lacking in address. Absolutely perfect.

Antonia had learned from her aunt that Mrs. Lowry's husband had died shortly after their first anniversary, leaving her childless and with pockets not altogether plump. Rumour had it he'd wed this penniless daughter of an old friend to save her from the disgrace of the poorhouse. Although he'd left her a small house and a modest income, she was still forced to scrape pennies together.

"Have you considered marrying again?" Matilda asked Isobel.

Understanding finally dawned upon Michael, and his gaze met Antonia's to share the jest.

Famous, he thought, though he smiled into Antonia's eyes, *another obstacle to consider.* This became more a tangle with each passing moment. Anthony Marley wouldn't believe it.

"La, Matilda," Isobel twittered. "I must do something if I'm to live in some means of comfort. Marriage is the only solution. . . if there were a gentleman to be found."

"Well, then," Matilda said with a careless wave of her hand, "tonight the fates are smiling on you. There's a certain gentleman here from the country, and I happen to know he's searching for a wife."

"Do tell!" Isobel cried, her eyes widening. She leaned forward eagerly, and Lady Hawthorne readily obliged her.

Minutes later, Matilda led her off to perform the introductions, beckoning with an imperious hand. Isobel, in a high state of excitement, hurried after her.

Antonia and Michael again exchanged glances, and fell to laughing. "How famous," Antonia chimed. "Isobel is *ideal* for Lord Wilson."

"She certainly is," Michael murmured, though a tiny line of worry creased his brow. The night was becoming a disaster. All he needed was for Isobel Lowry to steal Lord Wilson's interest from Antonia. . . .

The music struck the first note of their waltz. He gained his feet, bowing over her hand with an easy smile. "I believe this one is mine?"

Antonia placed her hand in his, a shy smile on her lips. She looked so beautiful tonight. This was the first waltz he'd ever shared with her, something he'd wanted to do since she'd made her debut three years ago. He would enjoy every moment of it. There was no telling if it might be his last.

CHAPTER THIRTEEN

MICHAEL DREW ANTONIA into his arms, one hand at her waist, the other clasping hers in a warm hold. His dark eyes held her spellbound, and Antonia became warm and breathless. Her heart fluttered painfully, and coherent thought deserted her.

Her dreams hadn't prepared her for the reality of waltzing with Michael for the first time—for his warmth, for his graceful movements, the strength of his hands and his cool breath fanning her temple. Nor for the devastating effect of his dark eyes holding her in utter bondage.

"This dance was designed for kissing," he murmured. "'Tis a shame the matrons wouldn't countenance such behaviour."

Her cheeks flushed and he chuckled. Antonia averted her eyes, fearing they revealed more than she cared to. Spotting her brother distracted her from Michael's lovemaking. "Oh, look," she exclaimed. "There's Rodney, and he's dancing with Maria!"

"Yes. But perhaps you failed to detect those brittle smiles pasted on their faces?" Michael queried. Maybe all wasn't yet lost. A feeling of guilt assailed him—wasn't he happy for his friend's progress with the woman he loved? Of course he was... if only Rodney would give him a few more days!

Peering closer, Antonia gave an indignant sniff. "Those two. I wash my hands of them. They're smiling owlishly, and aren't even looking at each other."

"And Rodney had the audacity to tutor me," Michael chuckled.

Alex Harvey swept past, the Honourable Lucy Davenport on his arm. He cast Antonia a smile and a nod. She returned the silent greeting in like manner, squeaking a protest when Michael abruptly pulled her closer and twirled her about. A moment later, she saw the cause of his actions: Lord Wilson and Isobel Lowry galloped past within a hair's breadth. Isobel's shrill laughter pealed as they ripped by.

Giggling, Antonia collapsed against Michael. "Thank you, m'lord. You saved me from certain injury."

She sent him a mirthful glance, and Michael sucked in his breath, his eyes darkening, before he adroitly reclaimed their waltzing stance. "She must have something in her eye. I've never seen lashes move so rapidly."

Antonia gurgled in agreement. "Oh, would that Aunt Mattie could see the fruits of her labours. They're a positive menace."

"She has," Michael said, twirling her about. "See her with Mr. Berkley? She gave them a killing glare. Lord Wilson nearly upset her as they passed by."

Antonia spied her aunt through the throng, by this time righted and shaking her head up at Mr. Berkley. Grinning, Antonia returned her attention to Michael. "'Tis as well she's a lively sense of humour."

"I hope you take after her," was his softly spoken, enigmatic reply.

The final chord of the music struck, preventing Antonia from quizzing him on what he'd meant. He bowed, offering his arm to lead her from the floor. Her aunt was at their seats, standing with Lord Wilson, whose eyes followed the departing figure of Isobel Lowry.

"Jolly good dancer, that one," he said jovially to Matilda. "Thank you, madam, for introducing us. Dashed fine lady."

"I see you've returned the roses to her cheeks," Matilda replied with a congratulatory nod. She sighed tragically. "Poor Isobel, such a trying time she's had. Not only did her late husband leave her poorly situated, he was too old to give her the son she so desired. Be kind to her, Delbert. She deserves it."

"Eh, what? Of course! I'm not one to trifle with a lady's affections, you know." He cocked his head to one side. "No children, eh?"

"None. Such a pity, too; she's so robust."

"Quite," he agreed, frowning. "Yes, quite. Servant, ladies." He bowed to Matilda, then Antonia. Glaring at Michael, he sauntered off after Isobel.

"He's changed his tune, has he not?" Antonia drawled.

"I'm to convey his apologies for his earlier rudeness," Matilda murmured, gazing after his departing figure with a positively sly expression.

"If you ladies will excuse me?" Michael made a gallant bow over Antonia's hand. "I anxiously await our supper dance," he whispered.

"As do I," she returned, sweeping her lashes with provocative allure. Michael played his part all too well. She wouldn't allow him to outmatch her. His keen gaze swept over her face, lingering on the flirtatious tilt of her mouth. He smiled, inclined his head and left. Antonia watched his retreating form.

Matilda's elbow nudged her back to reality. "You're wearing your heart on your sleeve."

"Thank you for saying so, Aunt," she replied, a blush warming her cheeks. She glanced at her card, finding her next partner was the undesirable Sir Reginald. She'd selected indiscriminately in her haste to fill it. She wasn't put about, however. She had no intention of dancing the set. Anxious to speak with Maria, who'd exited towards the powder room, she turned to her aunt.

"Please give my regards to Sir Reginald when he arrives. I must repair to the powder room." Waving a hand, she said, "Give him some excuse," and swept away before her aunt could protest.

Maria peered in the glass, resetting the combs in her hair. Her gown of icy green satin subtly emphasized the green flecks in her eyes. Her colour was high, and though it didn't detract from her looks, it clued Antonia as to her temper.

"Hello, Maria," she smiled. "You look lovely tonight."

"Thank you." Maria managed a smile of her own. "As do you. I vow I'm that envious of your gown. I would say 'green' but I detest puns. It is, however, most stunning."

"'Tis a gift from Aunt Mattie," Antonia explained, launching into a quick recital of its presentation. "'Twas the best of surprises," she concluded. "Now do tell what has you cross as crabs?"

"You haven't any guesses?" Maria enquired with sarcastic sweetness. "Yes, I see you do. That brother of yours! I could cheerfully dunk his head in the fountain. We must do the pretty, says he, mustn't let the tattlemongers gloat at our estrangement. I was prepared to play his game—anything to make things right with him. I even allowed him my supper dance—I can't know what I was thinking. Then he proceeds to act as if he's never known me past a 'good day madam.' Provoking creature!" She expelled her breath on a huff, sending the curls on her forehead dancing.

"I offered him the olive branch, and he's handed it back. He wants to play his way. I know precisely what he's doing." Tossing her head, Maria wagged a finger. "Well, he won't find me begging at his feet for favours. I shan't give up, but neither shall I grovel."

"Bravo!" Antonia burst into laughter. "Maria, you're wonderful! Exactly the one to give him the what for. I'll think him the greatest cabbagehead if he refuses you for the sake of pride."

"I promised to never accuse him of being a fortune-hunter again," Maria said, her own lips twitching with humour. "He said he'd thank me not to." She shook with mirth. "What a comedy of farces! I vow, he's not done dealing with me yet."

"That's the spirit," cheered Antonia. "Would that I could be a mouse at your table. 'Twould be vastly entertaining, I'm sure."

"Yes, indeed it will," Maria declared with a firm nod as they quit the room. "By the by, who are you promised to, Antonia?"

"Michael Alton."

Maria's brows lifted with interest. "Ooh. I saw you waltzing with him. La, Antonia, I made quite certain you were besotted with one another. You look a delightful couple, and Lord Alton..." Her eyes widened expressively.

Antonia could but nod and smile in agreement to the latter.

"Ah," said Maria in enlightened tones. "The pieces are beginning to fit. I'm the veriest dolt not to realize it sooner, though I did think it marvellous you'd suddenly made your peace with Montewilde." She slanted Antonia a knowing glance. "Would you be pleased to make a match with him, or do I miss my guess?"

"With whom?" Antonia asked with feigned innocence.

"The ravishing Earl of Montewilde, gudgeon. You can't tell me your aunt didn't have designs when she gave you that gown. And the way he's watched you tonight..."

Antonia hadn't the heart to admit his attentions were but part of their plot. "He's a far sight better than Lord Wilson," she replied evasively, thankful they were returned to her aunt.

When Michael claimed her for the supper dance, Antonia favoured him with a beguiling smile. Michael rose to the occasion with a devastating charm of his own. After filling their plates from the sumptuous buffet, he led her to a small table beside a potted palm, settled her with the utmost solicitude, and drew a chair beside her. Caressing her with a warm glance, he grazed a finger over her hand. "I've never seen you look so lovely as this night," he said huskily. A meditative expression flickered through his eyes. "Well, perhaps one other time."

Antonia's lips parted, a flush stealing up her cheeks. Inhaling deeply, she withdrew her hand from his burning touch and reached for a strawberry, biting it in a slow, bemused fashion.

"Unfair of me to say so, eh?" he queried softly. "'Tis just that I can't decide how I like you best. In all your glory, or... in all your glory. You're beautiful."

Antonia's heart hammered in her chest. He penetrated her guard, playing his part in a manner so sincere as to make her believe his intentions were serious. Almost. She strove for calm, taking defence in easy playfulness. "I'll be sure to give you high marks for this night's performance, Michael."

"I deserve them," he returned in the same light manner. "You're a difficult lady to make love to. You're forever changing tactics—I feel more engaged in a battle of wits than a flirtation."

A battle indeed, she thought. Her head fighting against her heart. "And who do you suppose is like to win?" she asked with a breeziness she didn't feel.

"You know I hate to lose. I place a bet on myself."

"And the stakes?" She sent him a playful smile.

His lips quirked in return. "A kiss... in the full light of the moon."

She gurgled with laughter. "Ah then, m'lord, it behooves me to decline. Propriety, you know."

"Chicken-heart," he challenged.

You don't know how, she thought, merely smiling in return.

By the time they returned to the ballroom, she thought they'd acquitted themselves rather well. Her aunt beamed approval; Lord Wilson bestowed more than one daggered glance. Alex Harvey looked none too happy, and the Honourable Lucy Davenport ignored them. Lady Bryson could scarce keep her eyes away, and the fashionable fribbles had their heads together in earnest discussion.

Later, when Alex bowed before her, she was quite relieved to surrender herself to his emotionally undemanding company. "I've been waiting in an agony of impatience for this moment," he greeted her. "You're the most beautiful woman present tonight."

"Thank you, Alex," she murmured appreciatively, smiling up at him. "I, too, thought it rather too bad we haven't been able to speak ere now."

"Your words gladden my heart," he proclaimed. "I can't think what I was about, not soliciting two of your dances." He guided her expertly through the steps, his hand firm upon hers. They were soon involved in easy banter, and she was unaware they were so close to a curtained alcove until he swept her into it.

The heavy drapes swished into place so quickly she doubted anyone had seen their exit. Before she could emit a protest, Alex drew her into his arms.

"Antonia, your loveliness has me captivated," he said in a passionate whisper. "I'm slave to your beauty! I've been in a despair of helpless jealousy the entire night, wanting only to be with you, yet forced to watch the other gallants monopolize your attentions. I've been fair mad with frustration, waiting for the moment I could claim you. And now—" he lifted a finger in a gentle caress along the line of her jaw "—to behold your radiance..."

He tilted her chin, taking her lips in a masterful kiss. Astonished, Antonia didn't think to rebuke him. She yielded to his expertise, allowing herself the experience. His great skill, however, evoked no response, and she placed a restraining hand on his chest, easing him away.

"Sir!" she whispered in light rebuff. "You go too fast."

"Forgive me, my heart," he pleaded, taking her hand in a more decorous pose. "I'm overcome by your beauty. Do, I beg of you, say I haven't offended you."

"I hope I'm not so missish, Alex," she replied, wondering at the urgency and frustration she sensed in him. How had she succeeded in arousing his ardour to these heights? "Of course I forgive you, but it's most unseemly to sweep me away from my chaperon's eyes. I pray it wasn't noticed."

"I apologize." He brushed his lips over her fingertips. "But should there be talk, please know I'll protect your reputation."

A tremor of shock tingled Antonia's spine. Was he saying he'd marry her? They ducked back onto the dance floor. Questions buzzed in her head, the loudest of which was why his kiss provoked no response. The remembrance of Michael's kisses—so full of fire and life—flashed unbidden. Alex, expert though he was, lacked vitality. His kisses were void of warmth.

Musing on this revelation, she glanced up. Michael, wearing a fierce frown, lounged against the wall beside the curtained alcove they'd just vacated. Had he seen her kissing Alex? He turned, making his way towards the refreshments. She peeped at Alex; his smug smile said he'd seen Michael, too.

MICHAEL SCOWLED INTO the shadows visible through Matilda's parlour window, his mind replaying the moment he'd flicked back the curtain to find Antonia in Alex's arms. Kissing him. Though hating to interrupt lest he embarrass Antonia, he wasn't inclined to leave for fear someone else might chance upon them. Had that been the case, Alex would have made the most of a compromising scene, and no doubt would've announced their betrothal on the spot. All to save Antonia's reputation, of course. A good thing they hadn't lingered, or he would've intervened. 'Twas well he'd made sure to stand out that waltz to keep a hawk eye on Alex's movements. The blackguard.

But why had Antonia surrendered to Alex's kiss? He should've been the one to enjoy her sweet lips. He'd hardly been able to keep his eyes off her. God's teeth! However was he to woo and win her—make her his wife? He could turn round right now, master a smiling, urbane countenance and ask, "Do you suppose we should announce our engagement tomorrow?"

But no. He needed an engagement from which she couldn't escape. And besides, his present mood was foul; hers, he sensed, not much better. Somehow their teasing playfulness had melted into gloom, leaving them both unsure of their position with each other. His scheme wasn't evolving as he'd imagined.

Antonia stared at Michael's back. He turned from the window to pour wine, looking like the weight of the world rested on his shoulders. Heavens, but she'd made a botch of things! She'd put a damper on Michael's ardour at supper, erecting walls whenever he got too close. Minutes later, he'd seen her kissing Alex. And he had seen, that she knew—his entire manner bespoke as much. What could she do?

Mattie had given her five minutes; Rodney had disappeared moments later. Her aunt had high hopes Michael would declare himself—'twas the only reason he'd been given a private audience. Had Antonia been able, she'd have escaped it. Her emotions had run the gamut tonight, from the absolute heights to bleak despair.

She'd run, guarded herself, denied and fled from the truth. She'd done everything but admit she still loved Michael, that she was as vulnerable to him now as three years ago. 'Twas not an easy admission. Was it possible to strike a balance when love was sheathed in the cold hand of fear? Did she dare allow it rein?

Michael lounged against the sideboard, brooding into his glass. He tilted his head, draining the last drops, and his eyes met hers over the rim. Her lashes swept down, shielding her heart.

He straightened, setting his glass aside. "I'd best go... I should hate to keep you from your beauty rest, though heaven knows you don't need it. I'm aware of why we were given these minutes. I don't, however, feel the timing is perfect."

"I agree," she murmured, thankful for the reprieve. She gained her feet, brushing against him as he moved past.

"Gads, Antonia," he groaned, his steadying hands pulling her into his arms instead. The next instant, he claimed her lips in a fierce kiss, demanding and hot with passion. She could but melt against him, returning kiss for kiss, knowing she belonged in no other arms but his. She could never love another, no matter how hard she tried.

He tore his mouth away, a muscle twitching in his clamped jaw. "I've been wanting to do that all night," he muttered. "You'd best go before I ravish you."

Antonia trembled against him. "One more thing, Michael. I didn't ask Alex to kiss me."

"You didn't ask me to, either."

"Yes, but I stopped *him.*" She turned and fled.

Michael stared after her, his brows lowering in reflection. What was she saying? That she favoured him over Alex? His heart stopped, then swelled. *Ah, Sissy-britches Annie,* he thought, *I* must *make you my wife.*

CHAPTER FOURTEEN

ANTONIA ENTERED the breakfast parlour, blinking her eyes against the late morning sun. "Hello, Aunt. Where's Rodney?"

"He and Michael left at an unconscionably early hour. Near eleven, I think. I vow I cannot know where these young men find their energy. I was hard pressed to drag myself from bed before noon."

"You enjoyed the ball last night?" Antonia enquired.

"Extremely. Mr. Berkley is delightful, but," she sighed, "I fear I'm too old to be thinking of marriage again."

"Nonsense, Aunt," Antonia laughed. "That'd be famous. Why, what shall you do when Rodney and I are gone? You'll be bored to distraction... not that I foresee it happening in the near future."

"I wouldn't be too sure about that, m'dear," replied Matilda, casting her a succinct smile. "You no doubt missed seeing Rodney actually *laugh* with Maria over dinner last evening, and you've been so busy filling your plate, I daresay you haven't seen your floral offerings."

"Where?" She glanced round, espying them. "Oh, do look. The most beautiful pink roses, and yellow ones, too. And three other bouquets besides!" Laughing, she read the cards on those from Sir Lawrence and his cousins. She paused to admire the collections for a moment, then turned her attention to the roses. "Ah, which card shall I read first?"

There were fifteen of the yellow, but the dozen pink were more lovely. She chose the yellow, saving the best for last.

"A token of my affection," she read aloud. "Alex." Inhaling their sweet perfume, she pondered if she'd inadvertently encouraged his fervent displays of warmth.

The matter didn't hold her attention for long. She reached toward the pink roses eagerly, and holding her breath, flicked open the card. A bold scrawl met her eyes, and she exhaled in relief. "How remiss of me," she silently read, "I forgot the full light of the moon."

Smiling softly, she fingered the velvety petals, then impulsively lifted the vase and carried it back to the table. Placing it in the centre, she sat down to eat.

"From Michael?" queried her aunt. Antonia nodded. "Those two are vying assiduously for your attentions. Did Michael speak last night?" Antonia shook her head. "No, I suppose it's too early yet. Did he kiss you?"

"Yes, Aunt."

"I doubt he would if his intentions weren't serious." This more contemplation than comment. "You'll choose him over Alex, won't you?"

"If there's a choice to be made," Antonia replied quietly.

"Antonia, don't give your hand to Alex if Michael holds your heart."

Antonia looked up, a brief smile lifting her lips. "I shan't. I'd thought perhaps it might be easier to give my hand and withhold my heart, but..." She shook her head. "I'm not sure I could face the consequences of such a decision. I'd rather not marry at all than marry where I don't love."

Matilda considered her for a moment. "You've always loved him, haven't you? That day at the millpond...? I'd wondered how you could hold your anger for so long. All this time you've been hiding a broken heart."

Antonia dipped her head, her smile sad. "He didn't know of my love; thought I was out to compromise him. His rejection hurt dreadfully all the same."

"Of course it did, child." Matilda reached over and patted her hand. "But don't lose hope. Three years have done much to change you both, and I vow Michael is in a fair way to being besotted with you."

Antonia wished she could believe her, but because of their plot—that idiotic, *insane* scheme!—she couldn't rely on the sincerity of his attentions. Oh, she'd no doubts he'd save her from marriage with Lord Wilson. But he hadn't promised to give her his heart and name in the process.

The door flung open. Rodney, followed closely by Michael, sauntered in, his face bruised and swollen. Both ladies' mouths fell open in shock.

"So that's where you've been!" exclaimed Matilda. "Rodney, did you have to allow him to batter your face so thoroughly?"

Rodney grinned lopsidedly from a fat lip, and winked with the eye that wasn't puffed and purple. "If you think I look bad, Aunt, you should see my sparring partner. I'll warrant Morton Smythe doesn't show his face in town for a sennight."

"Famous!" Antonia laughed. "I do hope you gave him a jab for me!"

Michael chuckled. "He gave him plenty of jabs." His eyes fell on the pink roses, then slid to the table where the other four bouquets reposed. They flickered to Antonia, lighting with a smile.

"Thank you," she murmured, blushing. Though she accepted that she still loved Michael, she wasn't certain she should show such obvious preference for him. Would he see through to her heart? "They're lovely."

"I'm glad you like them."

"So do tell," said Matilda, addressing Rodney, "how you managed to get Mr. Smythe into the ring with you."

"Michael arranged all that. Had it appear as if Frederick Halverson was going to meet him." He snorted. "He strutted up so sure of his victory, and when he saw me . . ." Rodney grinned widely, then grimaced and gingerly touched his lips. "Gads, I hope he didn't loosen any teeth."

"A pretty sight you'd make then," Antonia said, laughing as he tested them. "I'm not sure Maria counted on your being disfigured for life."

Rodney checked, turned hastily towards a mirror on the wall, then groaned. "Blast," he muttered. "I was supposed to take her riding this afternoon. Well, there's nothing for it, I shall have to cancel."

"Be sure to give the reason for doing so," adjured Antonia.

"What? That Smythe rearranged my face?" he scoffed. "Not likely, Sis."

"Oh, she'd think it ever so dashing!" Antonia exclaimed. "Besides, if you don't, she'll assume you're merely playing vengeful games."

Rodney paused, considering. "I suppose I could make *some* reference to it," he conceded. "But don't tell her he acquitted himself better than I expected."

"Well, but you did win."

"Yes," he mused with a smile. "Knocked him flat."

"Antonia, would you ride with me this afternoon?" Michael asked. "Perhaps we could invite Maria, so she doesn't feel too put about, and Lawrie Halverson."

Rodney scowled, then muttered, "Take his cousins with you." He fell pouting onto a chair, presumably because he couldn't go along.

His three companions exchanged secret smiles.

"That sounds a lark," Antonia said. "Rodney, do write your note, and I'll send my invitation with it."

"Do it quickly, whilst you can still see," urged Matilda. "I'll arrange a hot bath to soak your aches and pains and bid Cook make up some poultices for that face."

"YOU'LL NEVER GUESS who Lord Wilson drove with in the Park today," Antonia sang out, entering her aunt's salon after their afternoon ride. Tossing aside her perky riding hat, she smiled prettily when Michael handed her onto a chair.

"Isobel Lowry," Matilda said, sparing a brief glance from her needlework.

"She simpered at him in the most outrageous fashion. I declare, Aunt, he revelled in every minute."

"Trying to make you jealous," Michael commented, pouring a cup of tea. He looked a question at her, she nodded, and he filled another cup.

"You think so?" she asked, reaching for the teacup with a smile of thanks. "He looked perfectly sincere."

"I saw him peeping to see if you noticed."

"Oh dear," she sighed. "I'd so hoped he'd given up."

"Much as we'd like that to be the case," Matilda said, "I side with Michael in doubting he has. I received a note from him today, inviting us to a party he's getting together at Vauxhall two nights hence. He gave me a list of guests, and commanded me to make up the numbers, as he doesn't know many people in Town. I might've taken offence if it hadn't been so provident."

She smiled complacently. "I believe Michael, Mr. Berkley and Maria will fill the bill quite nicely." She tapped her chin with a finger. "That leaves me to contrive to get Isobel there also. She wasn't on the list. Perhaps I'll order Lord

Wilson to escort her—we've plenty of male chaperons. Yes, that will suit splendidly."

Antonia gurgled. "Had he included anyone on the list but himself and us?"

"Mmm. His youngest daughter, her husband, Mrs. Bryson and that spouse of hers who's rarely seen and never heard."

Michael and Antonia groaned in unison. "Mrs. Bryson?"

Matilda raised her brows in helpless resignation. "The night should prove interesting."

"Indeed," agreed Michael, sitting back on his chair. He peered reflectively into the depths of his teacup. Anything could happen at Vauxhall...even a proposal of marriage. But it wasn't enough that Antonia accept his "false" engagement, he needed something to propel her to the altar with all haste. Or someone. He needed Anthony Marley to drive home the deal, so Antonia wouldn't get a chance to back out.

Dragging her eyes from Michael's thoughtful face, Antonia asked, "Where's Rodney? Does he know of these plans?"

"He's resting, and yes, I thought it best to consult him before I sent round to the Berkleys'. He said quite carelessly that he hadn't any other plans. How was Maria today?"

"Vexed. He merely told her he was appearing out of sorts. She hadn't the slightest notion to what he referred, and tended to be a trifle miffed. I explained that his face was in some disrepair. She was concerned, and angry that he hadn't said so in the first place."

Matilda nodded her head non-committally. "Oh, drat," she muttered, "I do hate when my silks become tangled!" She bent her head to the task of straightening them.

Antonia caught Michael's gaze; his dark eyes sent a silent message. Her brows rose in mute question; he answered with a slow wink. Understanding, she caught her lower lip between her teeth and drew a deep, steadying breath. Vauxhall Gardens, the ideal setting for a lover's tryst.

She could scarce wait for the details.

As IT WAS, she still hadn't gained possession of the plan's intricacies when, masked and dominoed, she strolled beside Michael down Vauxhall's illuminated Grand Walk. They made a colourful troupe, Mr. Berkley and Matilda in the lead, attired in maroon and rose respectively. Antonia had chosen an icy blue; Michael wore a shade of midnight. Rodney, sauntering beside Maria, lovely in lemon yellow, looked dashing in a deep pine green. Antonia thought it a shame his swollen eye, disguised by his mask, couldn't be appreciated by his erstwhile fiancée.

She swivelled a glance at Michael, marvelling at how handsome he looked in his black mask, with the hood of his domino pulled back. He hadn't spoken a word of how he meant to order the night; indeed, not one chance had presented itself. Earlier, she'd heard him mutter to Rodney to keep on his toes, they would likely need his support this night. Rodney had smiled his understanding.

Tugging on Michael's arm, she now whispered, "Perhaps you might enlighten me."

Catching the hand on his sleeve, he squeezed it and whispered back, "Follow my lead. I'll play it by ear."

With that, Antonia had to be content.

Matilda halted the group, pointing. "There, that's the box we want." They mounted the stairs and greeted the rest of the assembled company. Lord Wilson looked ludicrous with his short, fat frame swathed in a domino of royal purple and a flamboyant, wing-tipped mask nearly covering his round face. Isobel, clad in gold, simpered at his side. Antonia stifled the urge to giggle, but communicated her amusement to Michael with a slight nudge of her elbow. He caught her arm briefly in return, dropping it instantly when Mrs. Bryson's sharp eyes turned in their direction.

Long before dinner was through, Antonia concluded that Lord Wilson was, indeed, out to make her jealous. The entire meal was a scarcely veiled flaunting of his wealth, each course specially prepared and looking almost too good to eat. Vauxhall's normal fare was ridiculously high-priced, so Antonia could only imagine what this might have cost. The sumptuous feast was followed by an array of tiny, decorated cakes, sugared confections, and an assortment of nuts.

That he'd gone to great expense wasn't the only clue she received. He'd seen to the seating arrangements himself, and though he could scarce remove Isobel from his right, he made sure Antonia was at his left. He placed Rodney beside her, and Michael ended up across the table. A haphazard arrangement, but then, how could she have expected otherwise?

Throughout the meal, he used various tricks to attract her attention, then turned and flirted outrageously with the gushing Isobel. His every action gave lie to the statement that he'd not trifle with a lady's affections. With Michael watching them, wry amusement etching his lips, and Rodney rallying her spirits by muttering whimsical quips in her ear, Antonia's sense of the ridiculous couldn't long be kept at bay. She found herself enjoying the absurd charade.

All were replete when Lord Wilson announced, "You may do as you please: dance, visit or take a moonlight walk. Heh, heh. Won't curtail your enjoyment by demanding complete attention. Wine's served in an hour, and then we'll view the fireworks."

He turned to Antonia, and she feared he would request a dance, or worse yet, a walk down one of the lesser lanes. Michael, with the quick grace of a feline, was there first.

"May I have the honour?" he asked smoothly, his eyes alight with humour.

Lord Wilson growled and turned to Isobel.

Antonia placed her hand in Michael's. "Certainly, m'lord."

Rodney offered his arm to Maria with a murmured, "May I?" and the foursome made their way to the area set aside for dancing. Matilda and Mr. Berkley followed.

Sets formed for a country dance. Antonia sighed in dismay at being unable to question Michael, for she was sure his keen eyes and nonchalant demeanour hid an Idea. The steps of the dance forced them apart. They came together again and Michael squeezed her hand with a reassuring smile. Her curiosity was piqued further. An hour was a short time for any plan to unravel.

The musicians struck a waltz. Michael swept Antonia into his arms before Lord Wilson could move. That gentleman surrendered Isobel into the arms of another and stood at the sidelines, glaring. Rodney maintained his claim to Maria, holding her closer than was necessary. Lady Hawthorne and Mr. Berkley seemed to be enjoying themselves thoroughly.

Michael twirled Antonia breathlessly to the music. She laughed up at him, but he wasn't attending. His quick, dark eyes scanned the area, and he manoeuvred her expertly to the edge of the floor. She looked him a question; he met her gaze and smiled.

"Your aunt is across the way, totally absorbed. Rodney watches us, as does Lord Wilson. Now is our time." His hand dropped from her waist, the other caught hers, and he steered her adroitly through the scattered onlookers.

The scandalous Lover's Walk lay ahead of them. Michael quickened his pace and Antonia hurried beside him. "What are we doing?" she asked, laughing breathlessly.

"Announcing our betrothal, of course. Is he following?"

She glanced round. "If it's Lord Wilson you mean," she hissed, "he's hot on our heels!" She tripped, and would have fallen headlong had not Michael's arms closed firmly about her. Righted in an instant, she found herself caught close against his hard chest. Instead of setting her away, he wrapped his arms around her, his mouth meeting hers in an ardent kiss.

CHAPTER FIFTEEN

"WHY . . . WHY," a familiar, outraged voice blustered. The lovers drew reluctantly apart to face their assailant.

"*Miss Marley!* You ought to be thoroughly ashamed! You're nearly engaged to me—" Lord Wilson slapped a hand to his chest "—and I catch you consorting in the bushes with another man. It's beyond belief. Disgraceful!"

"Sirrah." Michael's voice cut like a knife. "I beg leave to inform you that you're addressing my betrothed! You will cease your nasty spoutings at once."

"Betrothed?" Lord Wilson sputtered in disbelief, his mouth dropping open. "How's this? The last time I spoke with Anthony Marley, he made no mention of it."

"I can't answer for his failure to enlighten you," Michael returned, his voice cool and controlled. "Nevertheless, we *have* entered into an agreement, and if you should doubt my word, the announcement in tomorrow's *Gazette* should convince you."

"Well," Lord Wilson huffed. "That's the outside of enough. Miss Marley, my offer for your hand is of this moment—" he raised a finger, jabbing it towards her "—fully null and void!" He whirled on his heel and stormed away.

"I can see you don't need us . . . yet." Rodney's voice filtered through the bushes, then he and Maria materialized. He gave a tiny salute, grasped Maria's arm and hurried on.

"Congratulations," Maria called behind her.

Antonia breathed again. Her heart wreaked havoc inside her chest. Michael's firm hands on her shoulders tightened in reassurance.

"Now for the fireworks," he whispered in her ear. She appreciated the double entendre. He placed a strong arm about her waist, guiding her down the dimly lit lane.

A few steps later, a trilling voice floated through the air. "Haloo...Lord Wilson? Hal—oo! There you are, and dear me, looking cross as crabs."

Michael and Antonia exchanged glances, and crept stealthily ahead until the couple came in view. Michael pulled Antonia behind a bush.

"Come," said Isobel, coaxing. "Tell me what has you in such a wax."

"Isobel!" Lord Wilson puffed out his chest and threw back his shoulders. "I've made a most important and momentous decision. Will you marry me?"

"Oh! La, Delbert!" she squeaked. "It's so sudden. Why, we've hardly known each other a sennight."

"What matters that?" Lord Wilson demanded, grasping her arms. "You're healthy; I'm rich! You need a husband; I need a wife! We're meant for each other. 'Twas written in the stars!"

Isobel bit her bottom lip, considering. "You're right. Yes! I do accept!"

"Does Gretna Green sound as good to you as it does to me?"

Isobel's shrill laughter pierced the air. "A marvellous notion. I'd adore it!"

Antonia collapsed against Michael, laughing. "It couldn't have worked better had we followed a script."

Michael inhaled deeply, his arms closing about her. "I disagree," he said, his breath fanning her hair. "A script couldn't afford this much entertainment."

He brought her head round, claiming her lips in the most sweetly satisfying kiss she'd ever succumbed to. He drew back and stared into her eyes. "The moon isn't full, but I shan't complain."

He twined his fingers through hers, and they made their way back to the box in silent harmony. Approaching from the rear, they had perforce to sidestep a number of drunken young swains. The masked, hooded figure turning at their approach seemed vaguely familiar to Antonia, but her attention was diverted by two others, clad from head to toe in unrelieved black. They looked almost sinister, and she was glad Michael was close.

The noise from the box greeted their ears, and to Antonia, it seemed the entire company was assembled. She grimaced, hating to cause comment. There came a stirring within the box. "Why, Anthony! Do my eyes deceive me?" she heard her aunt exclaim.

Antonia halted in mid-step, clutching Michael's sleeve in sudden panic. "It can't be *Papa!*"

Matilda's voice came again, "Mr. Berkley, you recall my brother..."

A sense of doom engulfed her. "It is Papa," she wailed. "Michael, we're blasted. Lord Wilson's going to babble, and Papa will kick up the greatest dust. Oh, this can't be true!"

"Antonia," Michael whispered urgently. "Be calm. Your father isn't uncouth enough to get his dander up in front of a passel of people. Besides, we'd counted on this confrontation from the beginning."

"Yes, but not so soon," she moaned.

He drew her closer into the circle of his arm. "Come. Don't be afraid—it'll come about. Act naturally, as if our engagement is an established fact."

"Naturally?" she croaked as Michael led her round the side of the box. She drew several quick, deep breaths.

"We've just been congratulating Lord Wilson and Isobel Lowry on their engagement, Anthony," Matilda said.

Her father's appropriate reply came as if from a distance. Antonia set her foot on the steps, dread churning inside.

"And I hear you, Lord Marley," said Lord Wilson, "have bestowed your daughter's hand upon the Earl of Montewilde."

Antonia and Michael stepped onto the platform in time to catch her father's swift, narrow-eyed look, and her aunt's expression of astonishment. Her eyes flew to Rodney, and she was relieved to see someone who identified fully with the emotions she experienced. Scarce daring to breathe, she awaited her father's response.

To her amazement, he stretched out his hand with a smile. "Michael," he said warmly, "I see you couldn't wait to make your announcement. I'd hoped to be here when you did."

Michael grasped his hand, inclining his head. "You were. Lord Wilson just made it for us."

Lord Wilson's gloating smile quickly transformed into a furious scowl. Antonia knew he'd hoped to catch them out in a lie. But Papa, bless his heart, was a complete hand, even if he would ring her a nasty peal later. Matilda sent Lord Wilson a daggered glance, and rose to embrace Antonia and Michael. Rodney slouched with relief.

Her father gave her a warm, firm hug, and turned to Lord Wilson. "You see, m'lord," he said above the general din, "the announcement wasn't to be made precisely yet. I'd wanted to take care of a bit of business before it became public." He gave the man a telling glance, then smiled.

"Since my plans have been thwarted, I propose we celebrate.... To both happy couples."

He lifted the glass a passing waiter pressed into his hand. The rest of the company followed suit. Mrs. Bryson's beady eyes darted here and there. She positively bounced with excitement.

The noose closed tighter round Antonia's neck. Mrs. Bryson would babble, and she might find herself marrying Michael to save her reputation. As if in a daze, she accepted the sincere felicitations of her aunt, whose eyes misted with tears. Then came Mr. Berkley, and Maria, her eyes glowing with happiness and mischief.

Ah, the web they'd woven became more tangled by the moment, entrapping her tightly in its sticky, silken threads. How would she and Michael break this fake betrothal in the face of all this expressed joy? She was free of Lord Wilson, but even that relief couldn't soothe her guilt.

The fireworks began, and Michael tucked her arm through his, leading her off the platform. "I told you he wouldn't fly into the boughs," he said in an undertone.

"He'll raise the roof when we get home," she firmly declared.

But ten minutes later, when her father drew Michael from her side, she watched him go with trepidation. She envied Michael his composure. She made to follow them, having the greatest curiosity as to their conversation, but was jostled by the crowd. In a moment, she found herself divorced from the familiar faces of her company, and turned to retrace her steps.

A slight tug on her domino brought her gaze down to a young urchin dressed in rags. "Over there," he said, pointing to a row of trees. "Maria needs you."

She looked sharply, catching sight of a flash of yellow. Alarmed, she lifted her skirts, rapidly closing the distance to the trees. By the time she arrived, the yellow was gone.

"Maria?" she called, glancing about with a keen eye. Apprehension fingered down her spine, and she spun on her heel, prepared to flee. Two black-clad forms emerged from the shadows, the taller one grasping her roughly. She inhaled to scream, but a smelly cloth was thrust over her nose and mouth. *The sinister men,* she thought, and slid into blackness.

SIX MASKED AND DOMINOED figures hurried down the Grand Walk of Vauxhall with no show of poise or decorum. The night grew more sultry by the minute, a low grumble of thunder sounding in the distance. Maria clung to Rodney's arm, her face white beneath her hood, but no more so than his. Mr. Berkley supported Matilda; my lords Marley and Alton strode ahead.

"Damnation! Where is that man? He was to report to me immediately!" Michael fumed, glancing this way and that. God in heaven! Alex had stolen Antonia. He'd see Harvey in hell before the bloody villain wed his Annie.

"What man?" Matilda demanded. "I don't care about him. Where's my niece? We should've stayed, made a more thorough search!"

"She wasn't there, Matilda," Anthony said. "He's made off with her, but don't worry. Her life isn't in danger... only her virtue."

"Who's made off with her?" Matilda squeaked. "What do you mean?"

"My lord! My lord!"

Six heads snapped in the direction of the voice. Michael spat an expletive. "Tanner! Damnation, man, where've you been?"

The man stopped, leaning forward, heaving with exhaustion. "Couldn't find you quickly, m'lord, so followed them. Rode towards the southwest...driving a curricle...bays. A boy holds your black at the gate."

"Will someone kindly tell me what's happening?" wailed Matilda, just before she slipped into a dead faint. Mr. Berkley, quick to catch her, lowered her gently to the ground in tune to Lord Marley's frustrated mutterings.

Michael scarce spared her a glance, but whipped off his mask and domino. "Good work, Tanner," he said fervently. "Catch your breath and then follow me. I'll stake my life he's on his way to his estate—you recall the direction?"

"Michael," Lord Marley sighed, "we'll await you at Matilda's. I can't leave her lying here." He glanced at his sister and groaned. "Oh, Matilda, do wake up!"

"I'll have Antonia back, never fear!" Michael sprinted down the walk. Finding his black, he vaulted atop his back, tossed the boy a coin, and wheeled the great horse about. The black jumped into a run, scattering dust and clumps of earth. Michael scarce noted the indignant protests of Vauxhall patrons claiming their coaches.

Rain fell before he left London behind. His thin cambric shirt provided little protection, and as he hadn't a hat, water soon streamed into his eyes. He paid the weather slight heed. He had to find Antonia. Before Alex forced himself upon her. Knowing Antonia, she wouldn't submit to marriage unless she'd been undeniably compromised.

Rain stung his face, the blackness of the night stretching into forever. Soon the roads would be treacherous. Blast Harvey's eyes! Blast him to Land's End—to the devil himself! Leave him to choose this night to make his move—the one night when Michael was engrossed in working through his plan. The perfect setting, the perfect words... the perfect timing.

How had Alex stolen her so completely away? He'd seen the two dominoed men approach the box, but his attention had been riveted to Anthony Marley, his slight nod the indication that all was in order. Antonia's upset claimed his attention—he did hate putting her through such turmoil—and all thought of lurking figures had fled. He'd imagined her safely situated near Rodney when her father had led him aside, asking for complete details of the night's work.

Michael cursed himself for a fool. He'd underestimated his opponent. He hadn't thought Antonia might tell Alex where she was bound tonight. Harvey would pay dearly if he harmed a hair of her head. Michael burned with anger at the thought.

Alex wouldn't take her to his main house. He was cunning enough to know whisking her away so precipitously would raise a hullabaloo. No, he'd go to an outlying cottage, perhaps a vacant tenant's hovel, the gatekeeper's.... Michael hoped he'd catch them before then, otherwise how would he find her? He consoled himself that two bays and a curricle couldn't outdistance his black.

"I'm coming, Antonia," he muttered darkly. He checked at a sudden ominous thought. What if she'd gone willingly? His heart plummeted. Not his Antonia... She wouldn't—she couldn't! He wouldn't let her.

"Damn you, Alex Harvey!" he muttered savagely. "You shan't have her. She's mine!" The realization of his love for Antonia struck him forcibly. He lifted his head, shook a fist, and shouted into the driving rain, "She's *mine!*"

She always had been, he'd just been too blind to recognize it.

ANTONIA AWOKE disoriented and with a thick head, a sense of unreality nagging her. She recognized the jostling of a carriage, the sound of pelting rain, the soft, squashing noise of horses' hooves as they made their way over muddy turf. But where was she, and what was she doing here? She sat up in sudden alarm, brushing aside the heavy blanket covering her. Her head reeled from the effort, and she immediately lowered it, sucking in deep breaths of air.

"Ah, so you've awakened, m'dear," said a soft voice.

Looking up, she queried in bewilderment, "Alex?"

"The same. And never fear, you shan't come to harm."

"But... but why, Alex?"

He gave a caricature of a laugh. "Because, my lovely, circumstances demanded I act. You recall I invited you to the opera tonight, but you declined, as Lord Wilson had already asked you to Vauxhall? Well, I worried for your sake." He shuddered. "Anything can happen there. I paid a visit to your father, applied for your hand. He gave me short shrift, though I offered to exceed the settlement of that fat baboon he'd have you wed to.

"I had no recourse but to resort to foul play." He shrugged, drawing a yellow handkerchief from his pocket with a flourish. His lips twisted in a wry grimace. "I bought it off a Harlequin at Vauxhall. Worked quite nicely, don't you think? I confess to some doubts about being able to pull it off, but as it turned out..." He looked most self-satisfied.

"One night having you alone with me, and your father'll be singing a different tune. I hated to resort to violence. My deepest regrets and apologies. I wasn't perfectly sure you'd fall willingly into my plans, though I rather thought you might. I'm not being immodest, I think, when I compare myself favourably to a fleshy old man."

But he didn't compare favourably to Michael. "Alex," she reasoned with mounting dismay, "I can scarce credit Papa refusing your suit, but this isn't the way to rectify matters. I must protest this high-handed treatment. I demand you turn this equipage about and return me to my aunt at once."

"That, I won't do," he replied, shaking his head.

"If...if I refuse to submit to this...this preposterous idea?" she asked with rising incredulity.

A tight smile touched his mouth. He pulled an evil-looking bottle from his pocket. "I have ways to bring you about."

Alarmed, she shrank back against the squabs. Her eyes widened in doubt, a frown of uncertainty creasing her brow. Alex was behaving out of character. Gone was the smooth, flirtatious, carefree gentleman. Facing her was a man of extremely serious intent.

"Perhaps," she said carefully, "had you waited until tomorrow, you'd have learned I'm not to marry Lord Wilson after all. I was betrothed to the Earl of Montewilde tonight."

The news didn't seem to shock Alex. "Then you'll have to forget him," he said without expression. "I shan't be able to return you to London now." His smile was sinister. "You'll have to wed me instead."

Before she could utter a word in protest, the curricle was roughly jostled about. Alex muttered a gross expletive in tune with a great splintering noise. The vehicle lurched abruptly to the side, coming to a grinding halt.

CHAPTER SIXTEEN

ANTONIA WAS THROWN forcefully to the right. The bottle in Alex's pocket shattered, emitting a powerful, foul odour. Swearing viciously, he wrenched off his jacket and kicked open the door. Jumping down, he cast the jacket into the wet night. "Carlisle!" he bellowed. "Damnation, man! What's the meaning of this? I employ you to keep my equipment in good repair, not to drive like a bumbling fool!"

Antonia stumbled from the curricle, rubbing her forehead and gulping the rain-drenched air. The awful smell of ether stung her nostrils, sickening her. Holding her breath, she reached back into the vehicle, securing the lantern that thankfully hadn't been extinguished.

Carlisle wrestled with the horses, trying his best to soothe them, and whined an apology to his master. "I'm that sorry, guv, but this 'ere mud made it slide an' hit a rock. It warn't my fault! Whoa down there, beasty! Whoa down," he called, evidently at his wits' end.

Muttering darkly, Alex moved to help him calm the frightened beast. Antonia threw the hood of her domino over her head. Lifting her skirts, she fled back down the lane with as much haste as the slippery turf permitted.

The receding light must have alerted Alex. A short minute later, she heard his loud oath. She knew he'd be upon her directly, his long legs and her long skirts working much to his advantage. She bit back an angry cry.

His hand closed about her arm, wrenching her round. "You little idiot!" he shouted above the wind and rain. "Do you know where you're going? You could break your pretty neck should you fall down that ravine!" He pushed her to the side of the road, grasping the lantern to arc it over a wicked-looking gorge. "Now no more trouble from you. I've enough on my hands dealing with a broken wheel, frightened horses and an addlepated groom."

He pulled her resisting form back to the lopsided carriage, hanging the lantern on the outside hook. Grasping her wrist, he reached inside the curricle, bringing forth the long, yellow handkerchief.

"Carlisle!" he yelled. "Unhitch those horses! We'll ride the rest of the way. Be quick about it, man!"

He turned to Antonia, the handkerchief ready. She guessed his intentions and struggled with all her might. Muttering imprecations, he wrestled with her, endeavouring to keep her still long enough to secure her wrists with the hateful scrap of linen.

Suddenly, like a phantom in the night, a great snorting animal reared before them. Alex instinctively stepped backward, dropping his hold on her. Antonia flattened herself against the curricle, sucking in a frightened breath. The sweating beast came down on all fours. With a bellow of rage, its rider flung from the saddle and fell upon Alex.

"Montewilde!" Alex growled in tones of sheer loathing before sprawling spread-eagled in the mud.

"Michael!" whispered Antonia, collapsing with relief.

Michael was on Alex in an instant, his hand grasping Harvey's shirt to pull him from the ground. Alex came up with his fists at the ready, landing a solid right to Michael's stomach. Michael grunted, returning an uppercut to the jaw. When Alex staggered backward, Michael pounced on him. With snarls of long-standing dislike, they grappled together in the thick, slimy mud, rolling over and over, off the lane and out of sight down into the ravine.

Antonia's hand flew to her mouth. She hurried to the edge, peering over. The impenetrable darkness permitted only the sounds of their ensuing fight. She glanced at the nervous, shaking Carlisle, who withdrew a pistol from a pouch on his seat.

"No!" she cried, moving to stop him. He brushed her aside, muttering distractedly as he too slipped down into the ravine.

Another horse slid to a stop beside Michael's black. A big man alighted from the saddle, turning to her with the brief question, "Lord Alton?"

She pointed to the ravine. "Down there, fighting Alex. Carlisle has a pistol. Hurry!"

The man reached for his weapon and took the ravine at a lunging run.

Quivering with nervous energy, Antonia returned to the curricle, finding the heavy blanket. She couldn't bear to stand about doing *nothing*. She turned to the sweating horses and began rubbing them down.

"SO IT COMES TO fisticuffs after all," growled Alex, blocking a blow and giving one of his own. "Demmed handy with your fives, Montewilde."

"You've forfeited the fortune, Harvey," Michael grated in return. "You broke the rules."

"She came with me willingly," Alex panted.

"You lie," Michael growled, landing a blow to his eye. He wanted to kill Harvey for his desperate slander. The man deserved to be run through with a blade. He sent two quick jabs into Alex's stomach.

The night exploded with a blast that had nothing to do with flesh meeting flesh. Pain seared through Michael's left arm, and Alex staggered back, clutching his right. It took Michael but a moment to assimilate that the single ball had grazed his arm to lodge in Alex's. He lunged forward, taking them both down should the pistol crack again.

Back at the curricle, an involuntary cry escaped Antonia. Tears burned her eyes, and she collapsed against the black. "Please God, please."

"Fool!" she heard Alex scream. "Do you want to kill someone?"

"Idiot!" roared the big man, then all was silent.

She crept to the edge of the ravine. At Michael's harsh, ragged voice, she pressed a fist to her mouth. "'Tis well you warned me to watch for foul play," he rasped. "I've had a man following you for weeks. If I find you've harmed her, I'll be back to kill you."

"As if I've had the chance," groaned Alex. "Carlisle, you damned half-wit, get me home before I bleed to death."

Antonia backed away from the edge, trembling and shivering. Her domino was soaked through, and the only blanket at their disposal lay trampled in the mud. Michael appeared in the lane, supported by his man. He was splattered with mud, his hair falling in thick, wet clumps. His torn shirt gaped at the front.

"Michael, thank God." In spite of the filth, she ran into his arms. The grip of his left arm was weak, and when she drew back, he responded with a sharp hiss. Blood stained his shirt. She gave a dismayed cry. "You were hit!"

"'Tis only a flesh wound," he replied mildly, "but it stings just the same. Did he hurt you?" She shook her head in negation. "Come," he said, "let's hie ourselves away from here."

"What about Alex? Is he hurt?"

"He'll be fine." Michael took her arm, leading her to the black. "Can you take the reins? I haven't much strength left. Sorry I can't offer a side-saddle."

"I can't recall that stopping me before," she said lightly, concealing her concern for him. She addressed the big man. "Sir, can you help me up?"

"It's Tanner, miss, and yes, be glad to."

"My apologies for not introducing you," Michael drawled. "Tanner, help me up, too." They managed to gain the saddle, and shifted a bit to find a comfortable position. Michael put his good arm round Antonia's waist, drawing her closer. "At least it's stopped raining."

Antonia was surprised to find it so. The past minutes had been so fraught with tension, and now Michael's proximity nearly drove all coherent thought from mind. "Thank God. We'll be fair freezing before we find shelter as it is. Shall we walk, or can you do with a faster pace?"

Michael ran a hand down the black's flank, giving a low murmur of surprise. "Did you rub him down?" She replied in the affirmative. "Good girl," he said softly. "Let's see if he can take a canter then."

His arm tightened on her waist. Antonia lifted the reins. The black moved into a long lope, eating the ground as if fresh from his stall. The three made their way silently for some miles. Antonia was a good horsewoman, but found herself greatly fatigued. She gave thanks the black wasn't fresh, lest she couldn't control him.

Already a freezing numbness penetrated her to the toes. The only warmth she found was in Michael's body, pressed against her own. Was his strength waning, that he grew heavier by the moment? He swayed to the left, and she called sharply to Tanner, checking the black's pace.

"M'lord." Tanner shook Michael gently. "Look alive! We're coming upon an inn soon; give us a few more minutes."

"I'm fine," Michael mumbled, shaking his head. "Just fine. Tanner, man, I hate to ask it of you, but her kin must know she's safe. We'll need a coach in the morning. And clothes. Won't do to arrive in London looking like this. Can you...?"

"Of course," Tanner said stoicly. "Miss Marley can tend to you, and I'll find a boy to stable the horses. I'll borrow a dry coat, hire a fresh mount and be off. Got it all figured out."

"Good man," Michael murmured. "Antonia, do step up the pace. I've a hankering for a dry bed. I promise I shan't nod off on you again." He straightened in the saddle, but kept his arm tight round her waist.

The glimmer of lights in the distance was a glad sight. It was very late, yet the inn appeared merry with revelry. Michael swore softly, then apologized. "We'll have a time of playing least in sight. Follow my cue, and get rid of that domino as soon as we alight."

Antonia nodded solemnly, knowing they were in a fine pickle now. But she wasn't about to return to London tonight, on horseback, freezing, with Michael wounded. He'd run the gamut—a hard ride and a hard fight in the rain and mud. He'd endured a wound and ridden miles thereafter, all for her sake. She wasn't about to kick up a fuss.

Her feet hit the earth, stinging awfully. Though she shook with cold, she peeled off the sodden domino, tossing it to Tanner. She didn't care if she ever saw it again. Tanner turned, rousing the stables in a most authoritative manner.

Her thin muslin gown, although damp, had suffered no great harm, save for the filthy hem, but her slippers were stiff with mud. Michael's clothes were beyond repair. A fine sight they'd be, traipsing into the inn.

Michael gave a wry grin. "I'd put my arm about you to keep you warm, but I daresay it wouldn't be much help. 'Twould only wreak havoc with your gown." He paused, sighing. "We're in for a time of it, Antonia. You've done beautifully—no swooning, no show of delicate sensibilities, though you understand the implications of this night's work."

Antonia drew herself to her full height. "I'm perfectly cognizant of the facts, m'lord. I'm very sorry to have placed you in this position, but I do, belatedly, thank you for your rescue. I'm most gratified."

"I'm thankful I arrived in time," he returned quietly, using his good arm to pull open the heavy door of the inn. The innkeeper's wife bustled by, bearing a loaded tray of dishes. She nearly dropped them at the sight of the bedraggled pair.

"My good woman," Michael stated simply. "I am Montewilde. You'll be well paid for a room for my wife and me." He manoeuvred Antonia adroitly past the loud, raucous taproom. "We were set upon by highwaymen."

The woman's eyes grew round with wonder. "Highwaymen?" she squeaked. "Here? Land sakes, what's this world comin' to?" She stilled, casting a sharp glance at Antonia's left hand, her face wary with mistrust.

Antonia lifted her hand, glancing at it before returning her pathetic gaze to the woman. Her eyes filled with unshed tears, and her bottom lip trembled. "We've been wed but a short time, and my ring, 'twas so lovely. They stole it, and all our other belongings. And then..." her voice lowered to a tragic whisper "... they beat my husband. I was that sure they'd kill him. We were saved by a chance passer-by, but not before they shot him."

She indicated Michael's arm, and covered her face, sniffling into her hands.

"Oh, you poor child!" exclaimed their patroness. "And you, sir, 'tis that lucky you're yet alive! I'm Mrs. May. Come, I have a room, 'tis not much, but warm and clean." She hailed a passing maid. "Liz. Plenty of hot water. Our last vacant room is taken."

She motioned to Michael and Antonia, who sighed with relief and exchanged eloquent glances. "'Tis fortunate," she said, "we have a free room. What with this pugilist match in town, I doubt we'll see our beds tonight!" Wending her way up the stairs, she stopped at the last door along the hall. "You'll be pleased to note it's farthest from the taproom. I'm sorry to say it isn't our best, but you don't look as if you care much about that right now."

She produced a key, moments later pushing open the door. Antonia, peeking past her, couldn't hide her chagrin at the one double bed in the room. Feeling incredibly missish of a sudden, she glanced at Michael. His expression was inscrutable.

"I'll just stoke up the fire," Mrs. May explained, bustling to the hearth. "As you see, all is in readiness. Liz'll be along in a moment, and Dave, our pot boy, with your water. We run an efficient establishment here. Sir, if you'll give me your boots, I'll take them to be cleaned, and then, let's see . . . dry clothes, hot broth, brandy, fresh linen for bandages."

"You've been extremely helpful," Antonia assured her with an earnest smile. "I'm sure m'lord and I thank you most kindly for everything." Turning to Michael, she noted the trying time he was having with his boots. He uttered a protest when she moved to help, but she brushed it away, kneeling to make quick work of removing them, then handing them to Mrs. May.

The woman took them absently, murmuring, "Your names again, if you please?"

"The Earl and Countess of Montewilde." Michael sent her a fleeting smile.

The good woman bobbed a flustered curtsy. "My lord...my lady. Should you want for anything, just ring." She turned to the door, muttering, "Land sakes, an earl and his lady, and me too muffleheaded to recognize Quality when I sees it!"

CHAPTER SEVENTEEN

ANTONIA COLLAPSED on the bed, giggling with relief. "What a fine woman. It isn't marvellous she didn't recognize Quality. Michael, you do look a positive fright."

Michael clucked. "Villainous highwaymen!" His eyes caressed her, and he chuckled. "You were wonderful. I'd hug you if I weren't so filthy."

She smiled, walking to the hearth to gratefully stretch her hands before the fire. "I was prepared to swoon if she sent us back into the night. Indeed, I nearly did when I saw that wound in the light. It looks far nastier than I supposed, and it's still bleeding. Perhaps you should remove what remains of your shirt. They should be up with the water directly."

She tried to sound as nonchalant as possible, but her insides quivered in a decidedly queer manner. She didn't dare think of this night's consequences—that now, without question, they would marry. Even less was she prepared to face a half-clad Michael, tired, soiled and wounded though he might be. And only one bed.

"Antonia," Michael said meekly. "I fear I'm quite helpless, and though I dread asking, could you assist me with this blasted shirt?"

She turned, finding him thoroughly frustrated, with one sleeve half off his arm. The wet material stretched across his back and rolled in tight folds against his shoulder. "Sorry, I tried the wrong sleeve first."

She wouldn't be missish. She *would not* be missish. What mattered it that she'd never seen a man's bare shoulders? What mattered it that she'd never seen a man's broad, tanned chest sporting an amount of fine, dark hairs tapering down to a lean, taut waist? What mattered it that she found the sight utterly attractive, and devastatingly handsome?

Moving to his back, she placed her fingers in a tear, ripping the shirt end to end. She freed his right arm in quick time, but his left took considerably longer. The material stuck in the blood congealing about the wound. He sucked in his breath more than once, and finally, she stopped.

"I won't go any further until I've water to wash away some of this mess," she declared.

As if on cue, there came a tap at the door, and Liz and Dave entered, bearing two large cans of steaming water. Mrs. May followed, her arms laden with trifles which she spread on the bed.

"Here we are," she greeted them cheerily. "All you should need to make you comfortable, and another candle to see better by. Here's Lucy with your hot broth. Should you want anything more, please ring. We're at your service, my lord and lady." She bobbed a curtsy and bustled her charges out the door.

"Ah, what a multitude of gifts," Michael murmured. "Shall we start with the broth while it's hot, and you can explain how Harvey made away with you?"

"I wonder if he made it home?" Antonia queried upon being reminded of him.

"They had but a scarce mile to go," he answered. "I imagine they did. However, I daresay Harvey'll be out of function for some weeks. That bumbling idiot of his—he could've done serious injury had Tanner not tackled him."

Antonia shuddered, though the hot broth was delicious and warmed her insides in a wonderful way. The room was quite toasty, and for the first time in hours, she found the chill receding from her bones. She'd kicked off her slippers, and her crusty stockings were dried, though her gown remained damp. She wondered if Michael, still in his wet breeches and only half of a shirt, realized the same effects.

She related her story, her voice soft and bewildered. She frowned. "I can't imagine what drove him to this queer start. He was ever so nasty, Michael. Not at all the Alex I thought I knew."

Michael's angry eyes were hard as obsidian, his mouth tight in an uncompromising line. He tossed down his spoon. "Did that stuff give you a bad head?"

"I was rather fuzzy for a time, but all the fresh air cleared me. I haven't even a headache, which I was sure I would when I first awoke."

Michael's chair grated on the floor. Holding himself in stiff control, he moved to the bed, rifling through its contents. He couldn't believe Alex had put her through such trauma.... Yes, he could. Thank God he'd reached her in time. And what a relief to know she hadn't gone willingly.

He sucked in a breath, striving for calm. "We have here a pair of long flannel trousers which I plan to change into immediately. It's to be hoped I can manage alone." He quirked a lopsided grin, tossing her a voluminous flannel nightgown. "I suggest you follow my example."

"Oh, my gown is quite dry," Antonia hastily disclaimed, fingering the warm, soft material with longing. He cast her a disbelieving glance, and she blushed. "Oh, very well!"

Chuckling, he disappeared behind the screen. She dipped some water from a can, bathing her face and hands. Setting the water on the floor, she stripped off her stockings. The hot liquid caressed her cold feet and she sighed luxuriously. Having lost all her hairpins, she reached for a brush, listening to Michael's soft mutterings.

"Antonia!" he wailed finally.

Her hand stilled and she shook her head. "Absolutely not, Michael!"

He gave a shout of laughter. "I was teasing."

"Wretch," she muttered, brushing the last of the tangles from her hair. She tucked the tresses behind her ears, removed her feet from their bath and patted them dry. Michael reappeared, looking somehow even more destructively virile in the oversize pajamas. She grabbed the nightgown and ducked behind the screen. The warm, dry flannel was heavenly, but she cowered, trying to summon the courage to show herself.

Upon peeking out, she found Michael doing his best to bathe his face, hands and hair. Hitching up the sleeves of the gown, Antonia moved to help him, glad his attention was otherwise engaged. Lifting a half-empty can, she poured it slowly over his head, rubbing his hair with her free hand. The wash basin filled with filthy water, testimony to the accomplished task. She passed him a towel and he dried and brushed his hair.

"I feel better already," he sighed, raking her a glance from head to toe. "Pity that gown's so large. It hides your charms too well."

She threw him a quelling stare and he grinned wickedly. Their proximity forced an intimacy she wasn't altogether comfortable with. Watching him groom his hair with the same brush she'd used, his beautiful, bare torso constantly claiming her attention, brought home the knowledge that she'd share these and more familiarities with him. "You aren't making this easy," she stated drily. "I don't find compromise amusing."

"You were willing to go to those lengths but weeks ago," he reminded her. He managed to unstop the brandy and pour two glasses. "Here, you need some fortification."

She accepted without demur. "I hadn't considered what it'd really be like," she defended. "I find it very embarrassing."

"Would you have found it less so had you remained the night with Harvey?" he asked, his voice suddenly harsh. He tilted his head, tossed back the contents of his glass and studied her intently.

She struggled for nonchalance, but failed to keep her voice steady. "If I must be compromised, I would as lief it were you."

"Your vote of confidence gladdens my heart," was Michael's caustic reply. He scowled into the bottom of his glass, wondering what otherwise he'd hoped to hear. That she loved him? Did she? He doubted it. She merely saw him as a sight better than either Alex or Lord Wilson.

"What would you have me say?" Antonia queried sharply, her nerves strained to snapping point. That she'd be ecstatic to be his wife? That it would save them the embarrassment of breaking off the fake engagement? She moved to the bed, transferring the bandaging articles to the table.

"You accused me once of trying to compromise you," she said at last. "Then you went to great lengths to save me from a wretched marriage, only to find yourself stuck as my groom. Do you find it distasteful?"

She lit the candles, bidding him take a seat. She moved quickly in her agitation, returning momentarily with water, basin, and towels.

"Never distasteful, Antonia," Michael replied, pulling up a chair for her. Would that he had the courage to share his feelings! "Do my face first, if you please; I need more brandy. I couldn't have easily married you three years ago," he continued, "my coffers were far too empty. But I can now, and I'll be more than happy to. A man couldn't ask for a more beautiful, desirable wife." Would she understand what he was trying to say?

He studied her closely. Antonia's hand trembled as she dabbed at the cuts on his face. Try as she might, she couldn't force enough air into her lungs. Was it possible? Did he care for her . . . love her? Dare she believe . . . ? She couldn't meet his gaze, and instead turned her attention wholly upon his arm. The bleeding had stopped, but trickled again as she removed layers of congealed blood. Michael shoved a towel beneath his arm, shifting it to a more comfortable position on the table. His hand inadvertently brushed against her breast.

She gasped as if burned and rapidly adjusted her position, nodding mutely to his muttered apology. She'd torn most of his shirt away, revealing a smooth shoulder and powerful bicep. She was extremely conscious of his virility, of his warm arm beneath her gently probing fingers. His muscles bunched whenever he felt the pain, though he uttered not a sound.

"And you?" he murmured huskily. "Will you find marriage to me distasteful?"

Her hand stilled over his wound, and she turned quickly to rinse the cloth. Sensing his unwavering regard, she was careful to keep her face void of expression. What if he didn't love her? She couldn't chance laying her heart on the line. Not again. "'Tis as well we're to wed," she said at length. "'Twas distressing, receiving all those tokens of goodwill. Aunt Mattie was so very happy. I thought of the number of people we'd have to deceive, all the early gifts we'd have to return."

She shrugged. "It sat ill with me. I couldn't like all the false smiles I was forced to wear." She twinkled up at him, determined to lighten the mood. "I did, however, fail to learn the extent of your worldly goods."

Michael tweaked her chin, laughing softly. "I'll soon be a wealthy man. But you didn't precisely answer my question." Would she never give him even a glimpse of her feelings?

"I'm gratified to hear we shan't live in penury," Antonia teased, ignoring the latter part of his comment. "And now, m'lord, brace yourself, we're ready for the brandy." Folding a clean cloth, she soaked it in the spirits. "Do you want it all at once, or little by little?"

"All at once." He tensed in readiness, seconds later grimacing with pain. He clamped his teeth against a howl, then slumped forward, dropping his head onto the hand clenching the tabletop.

"'Tis a nasty wound," she ventured, sympathizing.

"Bind it," he grated. She wrapped the linen carefully, securing it with a pin. "Thank you." He stood abruptly, and Antonia made a pretence of tidying the table. "Do you think they'll arrive before morning?"

"I shouldn't think so." He moved to stoke the fire. "I doubt they'll *leave* before morning, especially with this foul weather." He straightened, looking suddenly drained. "I hope having one bed doesn't deter you from getting some rest."

She smiled tightly, but made no comment.

He sighed. Padding to her, he lifted his good hand, smoothing a lock from her face. "I was afraid it would. Never fear—I shan't accost you. When I make love to you, Antonia, you'll be my wife, and I'll have two good arms to hold you." His dark eyes probed hers before he brushed her forehead with a kiss. Striding to the bed, he flipped back the coverlet, sprawling his length upon it. He drew the covers to his waist with a weary groan.

Antonia sat by the fire, listening for sounds which assured her he slept. She was grossly fatigued, physically and mentally. It had been a long, eventful night, and she'd be a fool if she didn't take advantage of these few hours before dawn. There would be explanations and questions come morning, and in her present frame, she wasn't equipped to deal with them.

Finally she moved to the bed. Michael's chest rose and fell in deep rhythm, and she smiled gently. Thick lashes fanned his cheeks, and his sensual lips were soft in repose. She sneaked another peek at his wonderful, masculine torso before dousing the candles and easing gingerly beside him.

CHAPTER EIGHTEEN

A LOUD, RAUCOUS TATTOO beat at her brain. Antonia groaned, snuggling closer into her comfortable niche. The irritating rapping wouldn't stop.

"Antonia," a husky, caressing voice whispered. "It's morning. Time to wake up." She pried her eyelids apart. Michael's bruised, cut, and utterly handsome face rested inches from her own. His dark eyes smiled at her. "You're lying on my arm, so I can't go open the door."

In an instant, she assimilated that she was indeed on his arm, her head nestled against his chest. She flew upright. "Oh, heavens!"

She tossed her legs over the side of the bed, irritated to find the nightgown had crept up during the night. Her cheeks flamed. "Turn your head," she demanded crossly.

Michael rose, muttering, "I don't have the plague, you know." He moved to the door, admitting Lady Hawthorne.

Matilda's quick grey eyes assessed the situation, moving from her niece's dishevelled, improperly arrayed form, to Michael, whose lack of attire was even less acceptable. Her gaze ranged from his rakishly cut face, to his bandaged arm, to the only bed. She flattened herself against the wall for support, clutching the packages she held close against her chest.

"Oh, merciful heavens," she moaned.

"Good morning, Matilda," Michael murmured. "Can I hope you've brought us a change of clothes?"

"What? Oh, yes!" She thrust him the smaller of the two parcels. "Well, it's good you two are engaged," she said in a rallying tone. "I shan't swoon over this sight, I promise. I did that last night, and I've never been more sorry!"

"You swooned, Aunt?" queried Antonia with wonder, smoothing the hair from her face.

"'Twas most vexing, for we would've followed Michael had I not. As it was, we were forced to return home, where Anthony immediately demanded I retire. He didn't wake me until this morning, provoking man. Said he'd learned you were fine, so there was no sense starting off till first light. I was cross as crabs! Imagine allowing his own daughter to be fully, undeniably compromised! I've never spent such a night—I was so frightened for you, my poor dear girl." Matilda's eyes grew eloquent with sympathy, and she moved to enfold her niece in a tight embrace.

"I'm relieved you're safe and well, even if you had to spend the night alone with a man, and only *one bed!*" She clapped a hand to her forehead.

"Nothing transpired, Aunt," Antonia snapped.

Michael folded his arms across his chest as best he could. "Lady Hawthorne," he said in his most austere tones, "you can't think I took advantage of Antonia with her in such a vulnerable position."

Matilda threw back her shoulders. "I'm relieved to hear it," she returned in the same tone. "Now get dressed. Anthony awaits below. Thanks be to God! I don't suppose his nerves could handle such a sight. We'll have a pot of tea and be off; you can explain everything on the road. The landlady was full of a tale about the poor earl and his *wife* being attacked by highwaymen. Took a bullet in the shoulder. I was near to hysteria, thinking you were dead!"

A short time later, the trio, looking much more the thing, joined Lord Marley in the private parlour. While Antonia dressed, Matilda had helped Michael with his shirt. Though he didn't wear a cravat, and shunned the coat, he looked far more respectable than minutes before. His wounded arm was stiff and he held it carefully. Antonia's hair was neatly coiled, and she looked fresh in a pink embroidered muslin.

"Antonia, my child," said her father, rising to embrace her. "It gladdens my heart to see you well and none the worse for wear." He turned to Michael. "I thank you wholeheartedly, Michael, for returning her to us. After the rain, I wasn't sure..."

"Yes," Antonia mused, "I confess to being perplexed as to how you knew where to find me. And why, Michael, did you have Alex followed?"

Lord Marley fell into a fit of coughing, such an extreme fit as to have them all concerned. "Anthony, sit down, do," beseeched Matilda. "Antonia, dear, pour the tea. Michael, go pay your shot, and let's be quit of this place."

Michael coughed discreetly into his hand. "I didn't bring enough gold."

Anthony, still wheezing, fished in his pocket, handing over more than enough. Within twenty minutes, they'd given their thanks and goodbyes to Mrs. May, and settled into the coach with sighs of relief. The black was hitched to the back, and Antonia's question remained unanswered. She decided not to press.

The journey home passed in lengthy explanations of the previous night's events. Antonia mentioned that perhaps Alex's trick was due to a brain fever. Her aunt murmured a frowning, "Indeed," but her father and Michael kept silent. With the entirety of the tale related, her father sat back on his seat and folded his arms across his chest.

"It's good you're engaged," was his flat comment after he learned how many beds the room had. He directed a thick-browed stare at his daughter. "Your life's been quite eventful this past few weeks, m'dear. I almost had you betrothed to Lord Wilson, and he says he found you in the bushes locked in a passionate embrace with Michael. I arrived to see how you fared, to find you betrothed to a man who hadn't sought my permission."

"Had you been in London, instead of closeted in the country, sirrah," snapped his sister, "you would've known an announcement was imminent. 'Tis only too bad Lord Wilson had the gall to follow them. I saw them going, and believe me, had Michael not come up to scratch, I'd have made sure why. As to him not applying to you, I confess to finding it rather amiss, but I cannot know when he would've found the time."

"I'm not saying I don't favour the match, Matilda," Anthony said placatingly. "Indeed, I think it splendid. I'm sure my daughter will make a handsome countess." He glanced at Antonia, who made a show of studying her nails with fevered interest. "Now that the matter of a husband has been settled, we must needs move on to the details. After last night, I think it only fitting to insist on a very short engagement period."

"How short?" demanded Matilda in tune with Antonia's exasperated, "Papa, *nothing transpired!*"

"A week."

"A week? Anthony, have your wits gone a-begging? It can't be done. There's a licence to get, settlements to draw, a clergyman to hire, gowns, invitations, a ball. Why, it'll take six weeks!"

"I haven't six weeks," he returned firmly. "I have *one* week. And had you ordered the wedding gown as I bid you in my letter, we shouldn't have to wait on't."

"I did order the gown," Matilda replied, and to her stricken niece, "Never fear, 'tis gorgeous, m'dear. Still, Anthony, it can't be done."

"Nonsense! We could get a special licence and have them wed within the hour. It *can* be done!"

The carriage drew up before Lady Hawthorne's residence. The four alighted and entered the house, Matilda huffing that it was too ramshackled by far. "Come," she commanded. "We'll have breakfast and discuss this business in a sensible manner."

Antonia stopped short, suddenly at the end of her tether. She would marry Michael—indeed, 'twas what she'd always wanted—but he hadn't spoken a word of love. She'd managed to place him in a compromising position, after all.

"I don't want breakfast," she stated abruptly, "and I don't want to discuss marriage!" Her tones rose. "I don't want another person to say, 'It's good you are engaged.' I won't marry without a gown, and I won't marry without attendants. I *will* be married in a church, and with all my loved ones present, including Grandmother Marley!" She dashed an angry tear from her eye. "Now, I beg to be excused and left undisturbed." She turned and fled.

"How insensitive of us," snapped Matilda. "The poor child is overset. She's been betrothed, kidnapped, compromised, and heaven knows what else, and us harping about her wedding with all haste. Anthony, what a brutish thing to do!"

Lord Marley ducked his head in chagrin. Michael clapped a hand on his shoulder; the man had done enough and more for him. He stared after his betrothed's fleeing figure, a brooding expression in his weary eyes. He chastised himself for a lout, and more than that, a brute. Antonia didn't want to marry him any more than she'd wanted Harvey or Wilson.

A muscle twitched in his jaw. He wanted to follow her, confess all. But then he'd never make her his bride. To the devil with Uncle George's money. He wanted Antonia more than anything.

PENSIVELY, ANTONIA fingered the velvety red petals of the rose adorning her breakfast tray. A tiny note attached to the stem read, "To my beautiful bride." Her wedding morn—the day she would marry Lord Michael Alton, Earl of Montewilde. Somehow, she'd never imagined it to be like this. Her mind drifted to her hopes of three years ago. Michael passionately exclaiming he loved her, asking her to marry him. She'd imagined and discarded any number of scenarios, a whole troop of declarations, but in all of them, one theme ran true. He'd always told her he loved her—something noticeably lacking in reality.

The past ten days had flown in such a flurry, she hadn't had time to dwell much on that important fact. She was happy, nay, ecstatic, to become his wife, but knew a wealth of uneasiness at his neglect to assure her of his feelings. Certainly he was honour bound to protect her reputation, and he'd accepted that without demur, but it didn't mean he'd have married her had he a choice. Which bothered her.

A frown crept between her brows. His actions suggested he did care to some degree, for he'd been more than kind to her on their limited meetings. Having taken ill with a cold and fever the day of their return, he'd conducted his marital business from his bed.

Upon his advent from the sick-room, he'd presented her with a beautiful diamond-and-sapphire ring. She fell immediately in love with it, twisting her hand to admire its sparkle in the candlelight. She sensed Michael's pleasure and relief at her reaction. Tears had pricked the back of her eyes—for some absurd reason, she'd wanted to cry for a lost dream coming true.

Conversation, however, had been rather tense, focusing on pleasantries, his health and how his wound progressed. Only once did he mention anything about their forced relationship. Brushing a tendril from her face, he'd stated he hoped she'd never regret joining her hand with his, and he'd kissed her tenderly before she could reply she never would.

Again she smoothed the soft petals, her eyes resting on the simple note. She would marry Michael today, with all hopes that he loved her as much as she did him. Her lips lifted in a tentative smile. Soon she would be his bride.

Polly entered, lifting her hands in despair. "Miss Antonia, the entire house is at sixes and sevens, and I'll be that surprised if your aunt makes it to the church before she has an apoplexy. Your bath is ready, and I urge you to hurry, lest she come down on my head for not having you readied in time."

Antonia laughed, glad she was blessedly sequestered in her chambers, away from the hullabaloo of wedding preparations. The last days had given her all the taste she wanted of that business. Though it would be a small wedding, her aunt was adamant it would befit an earl and his countess. The planning required for such an event astounded Antonia, and she almost wished she'd accepted her father's suggestion. But Grandmother Marley was here, with her cousins and their spouses. She hastily finished her chocolate and scrambled out of bed, eager to get on with the day.

She luxuriated in the warm, perfumed bath whilst Polly bustled about readying her bridal garments. It wasn't long before Polly urged her to be done, for how was her hair ever to dry? Minutes later, she sat at her vanity, clad in her undergarments, applying a trace of cosmetics to her already blooming features.

Matilda found her thus, sitting demurely, her hair partially done. "Gracious, Antonia!" she exclaimed. "Make haste! We haven't much time and you're not even dressed!"

"They'll wait for me, Aunt," Antonia said with easy assurance.

"But a shabby thing indeed to be late for your own wedding!"

"I shan't be late. I'm quite nearly done, but I refuse to look less than perfect on my wedding day."

Matilda sniffed. "Very well, but do let's get you into this gown. 'Twill give me some hope you'll arrive on time."

No sooner did the silk-and-lace confection of white and silver swirl about Antonia's ankles than a tentative knock came at the door. Matilda rapped an order to enter, and Maria floated in, lovely in her shimmering gown of pale pink. Her glowing eyes and cheeks added to the pretty picture. Being Antonia's bridal maid, she carried two bouquets of pink roses.

"You look wonderful, Maria," Antonia congratulated her. "Has Rodney seen you yet?"

Maria gurgled. "He couldn't help it when I careened directly into him in the hall!" She blushed shyly. "He said he couldn't wait to walk down the aisle with me."

"Oh ho! He's coming to his senses!" Antonia laughed.

"About time," Maria said with a twinkle. "An odd thing happened as I came through your gate. A dirty little urchin accosted me, pressed a letter into my hand and said, 'Miss Marley, you're to read this before you marry his lordship'. Only his words weren't so intelligible. He ran away before I could inform him I wasn't Miss Marley... but here's the missive."

"How interesting," Antonia mused, reaching for it. She dared not move with Polly hooking her gown from behind and Matilda straightening it in the front.

"Not now, miss," said Matilda. "We haven't time." She turned Antonia in the opposite direction. "Now let Polly finish your hair and arrange the head-dress."

Antonia submitted with a laugh, saying over her shoulder, "Put it in my reticule, Maria, please. I can read it on the way to the church. By the by, the flowers are beautiful. I do hope Michael approves of pink."

"I doubt he cares so long as you marry him," Matilda assured her with a smile. Antonia hoped her aunt was correct.

She was ready a full fifteen minutes before their departure. Her chamber was bombarded with female relatives, including her grandmother, which served to stave off Antonia's nervous anticipation. Good wishes, affectionate kisses, and compliments to her gown flowed in abundance. Indeed, the light creation made her *feel* pretty. The low bodice and high waist flowed into a softly elegant skirt. A wreath of baby pink roses adorned her head. Her aunt's choice was impeccable.

Before leaving, she glanced with affection around the room she regarded as hers. A lump settled in her throat at the knowledge of her changing circumstances. "Polly," she asked, her voice somewhat shaky, "you'll have my things removed to my new home?"

"Yes, Miss," Polly assured her with a smile.

Antonia nodded. "Right, then. I'll see you there."

"Best wishes, Miss Antonia."

"Thank you, Polly."

Maria pressed a bouquet into her hand, and Antonia was bustled through the door, surrounded by laughing, chattering females in high spirits. The men assembled below-stairs lifted a cheer at her appearance. She laughed, twirled before them, and floated gracefully down the stairs to receive their good wishes.

Accepting her father's arm, she was led to the waiting coach. As it rumbled away, butterflies accosted her. She twisted her hands until her aunt admonished her to stop lest she spoil her gloves. She gripped the seat instead. Her father and Rodney chuckled at her apprehension. She managed a weak smile in return, but couldn't rid herself of her nervousness.

She remembered her reticule and the mysterious letter as they approached the church. The coach pulled to a halt, and she quickly dismissed her curiosity at its contents, leaning forward to catch sight of those attending the ceremony.

As she walked up the aisle on her father's arm, a curious calm settled over her. Michael waited for her, straight and handsome in grey, accented by a pink waistcoat. A smile played on his lips, and his warm eyes covertly studied her. He offered his arm and they stepped forward to meet the vicar.

Michael's deep, intense voice recited his vows without flaw. Antonia was thankful to get the words off her tongue with some semblance of her normal tones. They were pronounced man and wife, and Michael, with a tender smile, murmured huskily, "My countess, my wife." He smiled almost triumphantly, lowering his mouth to take hers in a gentle kiss.

CHAPTER NINETEEN

A WEDDING BREAKFAST followed at Matilda's, the festivities lasting until well into the evening, with much toasting and cheering of the newly wedded couple. Antonia floated through the day, awed at the knowledge that she and Michael were truly wed. Only one event perplexed her. She overheard her father congratulating Michael, which wasn't so strange, save that he added, "It couldn't have turned out better."

Michael, in turn, clasped his hand. "Thank you, Anthony, for everything. I couldn't have accomplished it without you."

"More than happy to help. Glad you came to me, son."

Antonia hadn't a chance to muse over it; her cousin accosted her, declaring she must have a word.

"On the way back up the aisle, Rodney asked me to be his wife—again," Maria told her in a shy aside. "Provoking creature! I couldn't laugh and cry and fall on him with kisses in front of the world and the vicar! So I settled for a mere, 'I'd love to.' "

Antonia laughed, giving her a fierce hug. "I couldn't have wished for a better sister. I'm so happy for you, Maria!"

Later, she expressed her joy to Rodney, who smiled complacently. "I think watching you and Michael infected me."

"I hope you don't consider it a disease?" she teased.

He chuckled, hugging her. "One I'd gladly live with my entire life."

Michael claimed her attention, offering a glass of champagne, and Rodney strolled away. "You've heard his good news? I can't tell you how relieved I am to see them together again."

Antonia tilted her head and queried, "Relieved? Not happy?"

Bad choice of words, Montewilde, Michael thought. He couldn't tell Antonia he'd have been responsible had Maria continued regarding Rodney as a fortune-hunter. "Happy, certainly, but more relieved. After all the brangle of the last weeks, I wasn't sure they'd ever come about. But Maria seems a young lady with a delightful sense of humour, which is well, since Rodney'll surely have need of it."

"No doubt," Antonia agreed, gurgling with laughter.

He grinned. "How good is *your* sense of humour?"

She gazed at him searchingly. "You mentioned that once before. Is it important that I have one?"

He inclined his head. "In the future, when you learn things about me you don't know. There'll come a day when I'll be totally truthful with you."

A frown creased her brow. "Michael, you're speaking in riddles. Be assured, had I sensed anything devious in your character, nothing would've induced me to marry you."

"I have some flaws," he warned in a soft tone.

"I know. But you'll have my perfection to steady you." She grinned wickedly.

Michael chuckled. His eyes dwelt on her lips, and darkened. His smile faded and his gaze flickered to hers. "Let's go home."

Home. Michael's home, her home. Her heart palpitated and she inhaled a quiet, stabilizing breath. The only answer she gave, however, was a slight nod.

Michael set their glasses aside, closing the warm strength of his hand over hers. Adieus made, they were ushered into the evening with much cheering, laughter, hugs and congratulations. The coach was waiting, and no sooner were they settled than it surged forward, bearing them towards their new life together.

Antonia found herself in a perfectly idyllic position, nestled in her new husband's strong arms. Her head rested against his chest, his heart thudded softly in her ear. She tilted her head, sending him a contented smile. He caught his breath, lifting a finger to tip her chin higher. His lips met hers in a tender, searching kiss. She savoured every sweet moment, revelling in the pleasure assaulting her senses.

The coach drew to a halt before his town house. With twin sighs of disappointment, they drew apart. Michael gently traced a finger along her cheek. "Ah, Antonia," he murmured, "I think you're as near perfect a wife as any man could wish."

A smile trembling on her lips was her only response.

He straightened. "Come. Please say I can show you the house tomorrow."

"I've no objections."

Half an hour later, Polly slipped from her mistress's bedchamber, leaving a somewhat apprehensive bride behind. Antonia, clad in a white négligé she considered far too daring, nervously awaited her groom. She snuggled deeper into an overstuffed chair, her gaze sweeping the pretty rose-and-beige interior of the room.

Her own perfume bottles and bric-à-brac adorning the dressers and tables loaned a sense of familiarity to otherwise strange surroundings. She appreciated Polly's efforts to arrange everything as it was at her aunt's, even down to her reticule on the bedside table.

The mysterious letter! She'd completely forgotten it. Crossing the room, she eagerly fished for the missive, hoping it would distract her from this ever-increasing state of apprehension. Her curiosity was piqued . . . Maria had said to read it *before* she wed Michael, she suddenly remembered. How odd.

Breaking open the seal, she skipped over its contents, finding its sender none other than Alex Harvey. Her immediate instinct was to rip it to pieces, but a sense of fairness stayed her hand. If he were seeking to apologize, 'twas only right she hear him. The letter was painstakingly written, a shaky hand vying with neatness, and she recalled his injured arm, wondering what it had cost him to put these words to paper.

Sinking onto the bed, she held the missive closer to the candle.

Miss Marley.

I feel certain you were given to wondering over my recent actions. I have an explanation, and it's my intention you learn of it before you're wed. 'Twould be a shame to enter into that blessed state in all ignorance of your intended groom's underhanded dealings.

Whatever was he going on about? A frown knit her brows, curiosity demanding she read further.

Montewilde and I are connected through our great-uncle, George McAlver. He was grossly wealthy, and we both stored great expectations by our inheritance from him. Years ago, he lost a large section of land to your father in a card game. Your father immediately entailed that land as part of your dowry.

According to his solicitor, Uncle George didn't cease to ponder how the land might be returned to his estate, and he hit upon a workable, if hare-brained, scheme. Since the lands came to him as part of his bride's

> dowry, he thought it fitting they should return through the dowry of his heir's bride.
>
> You were young and marriageable, and he had two nephews who also shared that happy state. The terms of his will stated his fortune would go to whoever succeeded in making you his bride.

Antonia's hand shook violently, whether in rage or hurt, she couldn't guess. She had difficulty sucking air through her constricted throat. She exhaled slowly, forcing herself to read the final paragraph.

> Victory, I made sure, was within my grasp. After all, you scarce spoke to Montewilde. But, to my chagrin, I underestimated the crafty mind behind the innocent eyes of my lord Alton. I know not what strings he pulled in his efforts to emerge triumphant, but I urge you to consider Lord Wilson's role in this affair. After much thought, methinks he, too, was but a means to an end. If you do decide to marry m'lord, please accept my condolences. I'd have written sooner had my arm permitted.

The truth of his words hit her with the force of a pugilist's blow. Her shoulders slumped, the letter drifting from her nerveless fingers. A multitude of scenes flooded her mind: Rodney's intelligence of her father and Michael discussing the match with Lord Wilson; Michael's eagerness to put their differences aside; his willingness to help her escape Lord Wilson's clutches, going so far as to apparently flout her father's wishes. Her question of why Michael had had Alex followed and her father's sudden coughing fit.

They had been the plotting partners!

She rose from the bed, snatching up the letter on her way to the connecting door. She slipped inside Michael's chamber, clasping her trembling hands behind her back. Her husband, clad in a crimson brocade dressing-gown, turned from the wash-basin, his brows lifting in mild surprise. Had his gaze moved first to her face, he would've noticed the warning signs. However, it riveted on the sight of her slender form draped in the sheer white négligé.

His breath caught, his eyes darkening in awed appreciation. Antonia realized the transparent material stretched taut against her breasts, and she brought her hands forward, thrusting the letter into his line of vision. His brows flickered, his gaze flying to her face. His easy, welcoming demeanour instantly transformed to a wary stillness, and he stepped towards her, removing the missive from her unresisting fingers.

"So your uncle's will *was* valid," she murmured.

His brows lowered, and he skimmed its contents, his face an inscrutable mask. Then he turned to the small fire burning on the grate, and without a word, allowed the flames to devour the parchment. Straightening, he leaned against the mantel. "When did you get it?"

"An urchin gave it to Maria this morning. I hadn't a chance to read it until now." Her voice sounded constricted, and she marvelled that she retained the ability to breathe.

He regarded her through hooded eyes. "I'd meant to tell you, but not so soon. I thought it better to come to a warmer understanding of one another before such news rocked our relationship." From his searching eyes to his rigid frame, his entire stance bespoke a tense caution. "Had you read it this morning, would I have stood at the altar alone?"

"I was a fool, Michael," she returned steadily, staring into his eyes. *Yes,* she thought, *I'd actually imagined you cared.* From the pit of her despair, anger flared, exploding into life.

"Yes, you would have stood alone," she choked. "I wouldn't willingly join myself to a blackguard. I'd as lief marry a highwayman! One of their ilk would've dealt more honestly. You scoundrel! How dare you use me in such an underhanded, reprehensible, *knavish* manner!

"Trickster!" she spat. "I thought Papa a villain—and Alex! But you beat them all hollow. When I think how you cunningly schemed to entrap me...oh, that I were a man and had a sword!" She paused, taking breath. Michael remained quiet and taut, his face a shuttered mask.

"I've endured much these past weeks," she continued with controlled composure. "The fear I might marry Lord Wilson, the frustration, the *desperation.* And 'twas all part of an infamous deception, designed so you could lay your hands on a fortune. How despicable!

"I couldn't wait to thwart Papa's plans." She gave an unladylike snort. "What a gullible dupe, I fell right into them. Lord Wilson's the perfect pawn. He's so *stupid,* though it seems not so much as I! You had it all worked out, didn't you—getting me into such a brangle the only conceivable answer was marriage to you."

She inhaled and continued the attack. "And the marriage! Aunt Mattie was astounded at how quickly you arranged the licence and drew up the settlements—from your sick-bed. Even I wondered at your stamina. But they'd all been taken care of beforehand, hadn't they? How confident you were! And my own father! I can't conceive how he could have entered into your nefarious scheme. He even rejected Alex's suit of my hand. It must have been a grand sum you bribed him with!"

"Your father needed no bribing, Antonia," Michael said quietly. "When I learned the terms of my uncle's will, I went directly to him. He knows of Harvey's reputation. You got a taste of the knave lying beneath his cool exterior. 'Twas either Alex or I, and whether you choose to believe so or not, your father looked to your best interests."

Antonia uttered a disbelieving laugh. "That's rich. Now you're saying you did this for my own benefit? Am I supposed to thank you? Or perhaps you feel your cunning deserves a pat on the back? You succeeded in deceiving so many people.... Even Rodney was but a pawn."

He straightened his shoulders and glowered at her. "That's unfair, Antonia. I'd have never deceived anyone had I a choice. I couldn't tell Rodney. You know he lets things slip. As for Matilda, 'twas your father's decision to exclude her. Everything depended on how quickly and discreetly we worked.

"I won't deny I need my uncle's money, nor will I refute the charge that I used every trick at my disposal. Lord Wilson, Rodney's suggestion of a false engagement, the kiss at Vauxhall... all were utilized to their fullest. Even Harvey's stunt worked to my advantage! It made further planning on how to get you to the altar unnecessary."

He drew a deep breath, expelling it forcefully. "However, I contest the charge that I gleaned any pleasure from my deceptions. I'd no idea why Rodney broke off with Maria, and by the time I learned the truth, the die was cast. I wouldn't intentionally hurt him; he's too fine a friend. It didn't sit well with me, having to continue when my future security might well be at the cost of his happiness.

"I've had to live with my conscience, Antonia, so don't stand over me like an avenging angel. Everything I did, I did because it was necessary." His mouth firmed. "And I'm not sorry."

"Of course not!" she snapped. "You have a fortune. I hope it's worth all the deception!"

His breath hissed through his teeth. "I would not," he grated, "have had to resort to foul play had *you* not pulled that insane trick at the millpond. You tried to trap *me* into marriage then! Perhaps now you understand how I felt. Furthermore, had you not borne your grudge for *three years,* I wouldn't have needed to use such tactics."

She gasped in outrage. "You're beyond anything! You'll assuage your guilt by placing the blame on me? It wasn't me who lost my temper and went tattling to my father. You were a positive beast."

"And you were a scheming minx. You very nearly succeeded in your quest. Had I not understood your intention was compromise, I doubt your virtue would be intact today! I felt the veriest cad. I could've strangled you."

A bitter smile traced her lips. "You've done much worse now, Michael. You've used me—the kisses, the pretty words—all lies. I hate you. And while we're making everything perfectly clear, let it be understood that I wasn't out to compromise you. I loved you, but you were too *buffle-headed* to see it. And be assured, I'd never have done the same with any other man."

Her eyes, hard as icicles, stripped Michael of coherent thought. His heart, which minutes ago he thought couldn't have plummeted any further, hit bottom. She hated him. She had loved him. *Antonia had loved him.* God, could he be any more of a fool? He hadn't known, hadn't guessed. Sissy-britches Annie was up to any prank...or so he'd thought. He'd severely undermined her honour and integrity.

"I'm sorry," he whispered.

"So am I."

He closed the gap between them, taking her shoulders in a firm grip. Antonia's head tilted back, her gaze raking his face with scathing contempt. A muscle worked in his jaw, and his eyes smouldered with black intensity.

"Antonia, you told me once you'd as lief die as marry me, so I'm at a loss as to how I could have otherwise managed the affair. Was I to approach you and say, 'Miss Marley, my future and the life of my entire estate depends upon us marrying'? Would you have condescended to speak to me? I couldn't take the chance, and I wasn't about to stand back and watch that wastrel Harvey walk away with you and the gold. I'm damn glad I didn't!"

Chafing at his logic, she set her lips in a straight line, staring at the hairs curling at the V of his dressing-gown. He sighed, his thumbs slowly sliding along her collarbone. Her skin tingled at the sensual pleasure.

"Whatever your feelings for me, we're married," he continued. "That fact can't and won't be altered. It may have been easier had the circumstances been different, but since they aren't, we'll have to do our best to work towards a better understanding of each other. I expect to be treated with as much respect as I afford you. Though I'll not beg to share your bed, there'll come a time when I take what's rightfully mine. So be forewarned." He tilted her chin, gazing directly into her eyes. "I'm not sorry for taking you to wife, and not for the reasons you suppose."

Antonia sent him a mute glare of helpless rage and hurt. Brushing away his hands, she turned and fled, slamming the door and slipping the lock into place behind her. A loud thud from his room sounded much like a fist connecting with the wall. She ignored it, throwing herself onto the bed. Pulling a pillow over her head, she sobbed heart-brokenly.

Michael nursed his aching hand, his head resting on the wall he'd just hit. *Congratulations, Michael,* he thought. *You couldn't have made a bigger botch of things if you'd tried.* Why hadn't he realized she'd loved him? Gads, he *was* a dolt!

Poor Antonia, she thought he'd married her solely for the sake of a fortune. Poor him. He loved her to distraction.

CHAPTER TWENTY

ANTONIA ROSE EARLY after a near sleepless night. One look at her sent Polly bustling for a cloth soaked in camomile tea. The maid studied her mistress's swollen eyelids, her face impassive. She adjured Antonia to lie quietly with the cool cloth pressed to her eyes.

Antonia did so, wishing she didn't have to think. It was painfully humiliating. Michael hadn't *wanted* to marry her, he'd *had* to.

Now they were truly and irrevocably wed. For the rest of her life, she'd live with the knowledge that he'd married her for money. She couldn't strike back. He'd brook no rudeness, and indeed, it wouldn't be becoming. He was her husband and appearances needed keeping.

Someday he'd demand to share her bed. How could she face such intimacy with composure and a grieving heart? 'Twould truly be a test, and one not long in coming. Aunt Mattie had told her of the desires of men, and she'd gained the impression they didn't like to be refused. A vengeful smile curled her lips. Ah, yes, Michael would come, and he'd learn how little he was wanted.

She removed herself from bed with a new zest for the day. Polly dressed her in a pretty yellow sprigged muslin, and arranged her hair. She applied a trace of rouge, a careful scrutiny assuring her she looked passingly well.

A soft tap came at the door as she was about to exit. Opening it, she found Michael on the threshold, fully dressed and shaved, but showing traces of a hellish night as well. He smiled, lifting her hand to his lips. "Good morning, love."

Antonia's eyes narrowed dubiously. She applied a soft, facetious drawl to her tones. "Good morning, dearest."

Michael's tiny grin was wry. "Can I hope you're ready, and willing, to join me for breakfast?"

"Mmm," she agreed. "I'm terribly hungry."

"Excellent. I'm sure my cook won't disappoint you." He drew her hand through his arm. They made their way to the breakfast parlour, looking remarkably like any newly wedded couple in love. "I'll show you the house afterwards, and introduce you to the servants. I hope all meets with your approval."

"From what I've seen thus far, I've no doubts I'll be pleased. Your house is lovely, Michael," she said sweetly. Only her father would've taken note of the militant sparkle she knew lurked in the depths of her eyes, but he wasn't there to forewarn her unsuspecting husband.

"It's your house, too, Antonia," he reminded her quietly.

Michael's cook was of rare quality, having conjured a breakfast fit for royalty. Antonia praised his skills with sincerity, and the meal passed tolerably well. Their polite demeanour remained through the entirety of the week, only once threatening to crack.

After two days, Michael hesitatingly informed her he must see his solicitor, and couldn't join her for tea at her aunt's. 'Twas the first mention made of money since their wedding night.

She nicely informed him it made no mind. She was well able to visit her aunt alone. Besides, she didn't want to distress Aunt Mattie about their relationship. Michael replied with a sigh of relief, offering tentatively, "I'm quite wealthy,

Antonia. I should like you to feel free to spend if you wish. Might I take you to a jeweller's tomorrow? I should also like you to leave off locking your door."

She cast him a swift glance. "You needn't buy me, Michael," she said mildly.

"I'm not trying to *buy* you," he returned curtly. "I merely wish to give you a gift. And I desire your door to be unlocked. Two separate things. I but said them in the same breath."

"Does unlocking my door give you leave to use it?" she queried cautiously.

He sighed. "Not unless you wish it. I ask simply because of appearances. I'm sure you've noted Polly's curiosity."

"Very well. I'll unlock the door. But I needn't any jewellery." A bright smile softened her words. She couldn't be a total shrew.

Michael's disappointment at her rejection of his gift fled at the relief that she'd unlock the door. He stared at her mouth, tilted up in oh, so charming a smile. How could he bring this woman round? He wanted her desperately. He swooped down, his lips capturing hers in a brief, hard kiss. "Don't look at me like that," he muttered. "It vanquishes my resolve."

He turned abruptly and walked away. A finger to her lips, Antonia stared after him, prey to a churning host of conflicting emotions. Love, hurt, anger, vengeance. Drat Michael's handsome eyes! How could she pierce him when he tempted her so?

IN SPITE OF HER PROTESTS, Michael presented her with a beautiful sapphire necklace and matching ear-rings. Antonia immediately adored them, and cursed her weakening resolve to see him pay for his deceit. She wore them at the end of the week to Lady Markham's out-of-Season ball, along with another of Michael's gifts, a white tulle gown, simply adorned with sapphire ribbons. True to his word, he hadn't crossed her threshold, but she'd noticed his admiring perusal on increasing occasions. Her fingers stretched like kitten claws inside her white kid gloves. Tonight she would have her revenge.

There was one guest at the ball she disliked to see. Alex Harvey held court to a bevy of admirers. He nursed his right arm at a tender angle, and the trace of a rakish cut outlined his left eye. 'Twas difficult not to overhear his recital of a tale about being attacked by highwaymen.

"Wretched liar," Antonia murmured behind her fan, as she and Michael skirted the throng.

"You didn't expect the truth?" Michael queried. "Just as well, since your reputation would suffer otherwise."

She nodded at this logic. They were joined by Rodney and Maria, Matilda and Mr. Berkley. Antonia found it difficult to maintain her façade of the happy bride round her loved ones, but tonight the attention was off them, and focused upon the other two glowing couples. Matilda, waving her left hand where reposed a brilliant diamond, disclosed the announcement of her and Mr. Berkley's nuptial plans.

"Imagine, he'd been afraid to ask me," she confided to her niece. Antonia, delighted, hugged her.

The three couples soon took their places in a country dance. Later, in search of a glass of orgeat, Antonia was accosted by Alex Harvey.

"Good evening, Countess," he purred. "Your new husband's deserted you so soon? How quickly palls the magic of that blessed state of marriage."

"On the contrary, Mr. Harvey," she replied mildly, refusing to be baited. "My husband and I are quite happy."

"'Odso? Despite his treachery?"

He was seeking her confession that he'd wreaked havoc between Michael and herself, and she refused to give him satisfaction. "I *chose* to marry my husband, Mr. Harvey. I sincerely doubt any other would be man enough for me." She directed him a haughty look. "Michael numbers among the finest, and he is also *exceedingly* rich."

His eyes narrowed with malice. "You confess you covet his money, though he used you to get it."

"You're mistaken. I love my husband as well as he does me. 'Tis why he beat you so soundly."

Harvey's lips twisted in a sneer. "I wish you well of each other. For myself, I received a tidy consolation prize from Uncle George, and I couldn't be more convinced I've been saved from a fate worse than death."

"Remarkable how alike we think on that head." She tapped his hand with her fan, her smile sweetly sarcastic. "Good evening, Mr. Harvey." She turned, floating gracefully away.

Michael stood beside her aunt and Mrs. Hadley. "I believe we're promised for this waltz?" she asked, beaming at him.

A fleeting lift of his brows betrayed Michael's surprise. He inclined his head. "And so we were," he replied, catching her hand. They twirled in silence for some moments. "Do tell."

"That wretch, Alex Harvey," she readily obliged him. "He tried to wrangle a confession that he'd succeeded in making a mess of our marriage. I told him you love me—" she favoured him with a glittering smile "—so please, act as if you do."

"You realize you're giving me leave to express my affection." His grin was wicked. His eyes, however, spoke his earnestness.

She smiled. Like a cat, stalking its prey.

He twirled her faster to the music. They reached the open doors leading to the garden, and she realized he'd purposefully manoeuvred her in this direction.

"Sneak," she accused as he twirled her through them. "You didn't hesitate to grasp your chance."

"He's watching us. You want him to believe we adore each other. What better way than by disappearing into the moonlit garden?"

Deeper into the shadows he led her, away from the strolling couples, until he found a secluded alcove. She guessed his intentions and warred over whether or not to deny him. Then his arms closed round her and his mouth met hers. Unprepared for the torrent of desire cascading through her, Antonia melted against him, surrendering to the force of feeling his caresses aroused. Reluctant to withdraw from his heady embrace, she pulled his roving lips from her jaw back to her mouth, drinking deeply from the well of his passion.

At length he set her away and took her hand. "Come, we're going home."

Their coach appeared post-haste. A brief good night and thank you, and their hostess shooed them away, laughing. "Spring 'em," Michael ordered his man, and settled against the squabs with his wife in his arms.

Although it was imperative that she not allow his kisses to penetrate her defences, Antonia found it difficult when every bone in her body melted into liquid gold. His hot, drugging kisses left her without strength to hold up her head. But she'd spun her web, and he was helpless in its sticky threads. And oh, how he'd played with her heart!

Not a word passed as he helped her from the coach. Taking her hand, he led her into the house, instructed the butler to lock up and continued on his way. Polly waited in Antonia's chamber, but Michael communicated that her services weren't needed. Her face politely expressionless, she bobbed a curtsy and left.

Michael lifted Antonia's hair, blazing a trail of tantalizing kisses down her neck whilst unclasping her necklace. Inhaling slowly and deeply, she turned her own attention to the ear-rings, dropping them into his palm. He tossed them towards the bureau. Unhooking her gown, he rained sweet kisses on her neck and shoulders. The gown slipped past her waist. She drew another deep breath, quelled her desire and summoned every ounce of her courage.

She turned, a polite smile on her face. "Thank you, Michael. I can manage from here.... Good night."

She pretended not to notice the blank amazement registering on his face, or his brows snapping over eyes blackened with rage. Forcing nonchalance, she stepped out of her gown and lifted trembling fingers to her lace stays. She awaited his further reaction with something akin to dread. It was extremely difficult to appear unaffected when he turned and stalked through the connecting door.

He was back before she could pull a filmy pink négligé over her head. His eyes snapped with fury, and hastily she settled the gown over her naked limbs, swallowing hard.

"And you branded me a trickster," he muttered. "Seems we're well suited." He left, slamming the door with a crashing force.

THE BREAKFAST PARLOUR was empty the next morning. Antonia's heart sank. She desired nothing but a cup of coffee, but when she reached for the pot, her hand froze. A note rested on a small silver salver next to it. She tore it open, reading the curt, brief message. "I'll be gone for the day."

She crumpled the paper and moved mechanically to the grate, tossing it inside. Dejected, she watched the low fire consume it. Revenge wasn't sweet. She poured coffee, and cradled the cup between her palms, staring into its murky depths.

Her future stretched like a gaping cavity. Today was but the beginning of a pattern for the years ahead. Michael would avoid her, taking refuge in his clubs and other pursuits. And what would she become? Oh, to be sure, he'd want an heir, and perhaps being the mother of his children would fill the void in her life. She somehow doubted, though, that anything but knowing the love of her husband could permeate her emptiness.

Swallowing her coffee, she rose. She'd not wait about until she withered for lack of love. Smoothing her hands down the skirt of her morning gown, she exited the parlour in search of the butler.

"Please see the coach brought round in half an hour," she instructed, then hurried up the stairs. Bursting into her chamber, she shut the door and stripped off her gown. "Polly, pack a portmanteau, and be quick about it. We're going to my father's. We shan't need much, toiletries and a change of clothes. We'll send for the rest later."

Polly sent her a baffled look, shook her head and did her bidding. Antonia snatched a pine green travelling dress from the wardrobe and was into it before her maid could help. She grabbed the matching hat, and reached for her reticule. Her shoulders slumped. "Blast! I haven't any money."

Whirling about, she crossed to the connecting door and entered Michael's room. She searched about, opening drawers, finding reward in a ten-pound note and some coins. She scribbled a note at his desk, informing him she was the thief, and would soon send for more.

Twenty minutes later, with Polly in tow, she was on her way out of London, her shoulders squared with resolve. Hours later, she stared at the edifice of her former home.

Her chin trembled at what had passed since the day she'd left in the company of Rodney and Michael.

Fellows met her at the door. "Why, Miss Antonia! Er, excuse me... Lady Montewilde." He bowed deferentially, then grinned, and nodded at Polly. "I see becoming a countess has made you observe the proprieties."

Antonia laughed. "It's good to be back, Fellows. You know Polly. See her settled and direct the coachman to the stables."

Looking up, she espied her father emerging from his study. Hot tears pricked her eyes. Straightening her shoulders, she lifted her chin, sending him a militant glance.

He regarded her with some dismay. "Hello, Daughter. Do come to my study. Fellows, bring us something to drink... something stiff."

CHAPTER TWENTY-ONE

ANTONIA FOLLOWED her father, selecting a stuffed chair away from his desk. "You've made some changes, I see. New drapes, new carpets. Very nice. Fellows looks natty in his new livery, and you must've engaged more servants. Things appear much tidier."

"Yes, well, my children have made good matches. Besides, Rodney wishes to marry here, in the chapel, and we can't have his bride brought to a heap of stones. I've been working hard to see all is in order by midsummer."

"You've accomplished much in just a *week.*" The compliment could have easily been misconstrued for a charge.

He coughed uncomfortably. "Yes, well, I've been working hard, as I say." He met the discreet tapping at the door with a sigh of relief. Fellows entered with a brandy decanter and two glasses, placing them on the desk before withdrawing. Lord Marley poured out goodly amounts, placed one in his daughter's hand and, cradling the other, chose a chair.

"Tell me, Papa, how deep in the suds were you?" Antonia asked, lifting the amber liquid to her lips.

He sighed heavily, swallowing a good portion of his brandy before answering. "Perhaps, Antonia, you'll quit playing cat and mouse with me, and state your business."

"I know everything. Alex Harvey wrote me a letter. I read it on my wedding night. It wasn't difficult to put all the pieces together. You played me for a fool, Papa. How badly did you need Michael's money?" She found it difficult to keep the tears at bay and choked back a few swallows of brandy.

He winced. "What does it matter, Antonia? Would it be any easier for you to forgive me if I said I was ready for debtor's prison? But I shan't lie; I didn't need his settlement at all. I was merely trying to save every farthing I could to put this house in order for Rodney and his bride. I wanted to have it completed by autumn."

"Then *why?*" she cried, coming to her feet. "Don't you care about *me?*" The tears fell and she quickly turned away.

Her father's hands rested lightly on her shoulders. "I care about you very much, Daughter," he said gently. "That's why I did what I felt was right."

She whirled round, searching his face with tear-filled eyes. "Right? Papa, I was used. Did you never consider that a little honesty might be in order?"

"Sit down, Antonia." He refilled her glass and returned it to her hand, then drew a deep breath. "I'd no choice in the matter. 'Twas either Michael or Alex, and though I reside in the country, I'm not totally ignorant of Harvey's reputation. I wasn't going to allow my daughter to marry such a scoundrel.

"Michael had no choice either, save for backing out and letting Harvey have his way. Gads, *I* would've paid *him* not to do so! As it was, he was most unwilling to give in without a fight."

"Papa, this is confusing. Why couldn't someone simply tell me the terms of the will? I certainly would have refused Alex's suit, and Michael could easily have backed out."

"It's more complex than that. The will stated that if neither of them succeeded in marrying you, the money would go to a farm for indigent animals. Do you have any idea how large a fortune it is?"

"Well, no," she replied, frowning. "Michael led me to believe he's now quite wealthy."

He gave an emphatic nod. "Enormously wealthy. Far more wealthy than our fat neighbour, in fact. Antonia, he couldn't lightly turn his back on't! Now speaking of in the suds, his family fortune had dwindled for generations—a great-grandfather was a loose screw and dipped deep into the coffers. Though his own father tried hard, he couldn't make many advances. 'Tis a huge estate, and things do fall into disrepair. Michael was raised with an eye to his responsibilities. The welfare of easily hundreds of people lies on his shoulders."

Antonia drained her glass for the second time and set it down smartly on the table beside her. "Well, thank you, Papa, for your enlightenment. You've succeeded in making me feel insufferably selfish! Why didn't I give thought to his tenants and farms? No, all I thought of was how he'd used me. I tried so hard not to fall in love with him again, and fool that I was, I thought he cared...."

Rising, she snatched up her glass to refill it again, but a slight dizziness in her head cautioned her to go easy. "Do you know how terribly it hurts to know he only wanted me so he could lay his hands on a fortune?"

Lord Marley's face was the picture of compassion. "I'm sorry... I didn't know. Did Michael?"

She shook her head.

"How could he have known?" he asked. "You were so cool and aloof, I made sure you didn't care one whit. I thought you held a grudge because he tattled about the millpond." He fell back in his chair, lifting his eyes heavenward. "The *millpond.* I begin to perceive it was more than a youngsters' squabble. Perhaps you should tell me your side of it."

Heaving a doleful sigh, Antonia relayed her tale as succinctly as possible, finishing with an injured sniff. "I tried to hate him, but I never really succeeded, though I told him I did so on our wedding night."

Her father stared at the ceiling, thoughtfully rubbing his chin. "This letter from Harvey. You say you didn't read it until…er, before—" He frowned then asked directly, "Has your marriage been consummated?"

She shook her head. "No, and likely never will be."

He glanced at her sharply. She lifted her brows expressively. He sighed. "I don't believe I want to know the details."

"No, you don't. Suffice it to say I discovered a way to get back," she said in a tiny voice. "That was last night. He was gone this morning." She blinked rapidly. "I shan't wait about watching him hate me every day."

"Ah, Antonia, I fear Michael will have to pay for every pound of that fortune, for a biddable wife he certainly didn't get." Lord Marley shook his head, the ghost of a smile on his lips. "You tell me you love him and have for some time. How strong is your love? Can you love him despite what he's done? If your marriage isn't consummated, you could have it annulled."

She froze at the thought.

Her father continued. "I don't think there'd be any threat of Michael losing the inheritance. The lands have been legally returned to the estate, and the will didn't mention having to produce an heir, so that shouldn't stand in your way. However, he didn't marry you under false pretenses, as you were compromised, and he's never told you he loved you. But I'm sure that wily solicitor can find a way round it."

He paused, considering her carefully. "Before you come to any decision, there are things you should know. Michael had no need to marry you." At her incredulous expression, he inclined his head. "The moment Alex whisked you away, he broke the terms of the will, and therefore forfeited the fortune. In fact, there was no need for Michael to even ride after you that night. The inheritance was already his.

"I know he doubted Harvey's integrity, and with every right. Once that man learned of his forfeit, he'd have left you to face a ruined reputation, with no chance of redeeming yourself." He paused, his words hovering in the silent room. "I can't guess at Michael's feelings for you, but I have every cause to thank him," he said quietly, "for his good sense in having a man following Harvey, for riding after you in a rainstorm in the dead of night, for fighting for your honour, for returning you safely. I can't thank him enough, and you might closely consider these things before you rush into any decision."

Antonia sank onto the chair, resting her chin on an upturned palm. She shuddered at the idea of annulment. She was Michael's wife, had waited long to be so. She cringed to think of her husband ripped from her for the sake of pride. Hadn't she told Maria of Rodney, "I shall think him the greatest cabbagehead if he refuses you for the sake of pride!" Could she do the same, casting away the splendid jewel of love? She could not.

Humbled, she asked, "Papa, will you loan me a team? I must return to London. I fear I neglected to tell Michael where I was bound."

He smiled widely, gaining his feet. "The coach shall be at your disposal in half an hour, m'lady."

She flew into his arms. "Thank you, Papa—for everything. I do love him so, and I'll be a good, biddable wife."

"Don't make rash promises, Daughter," he cautioned, hugging her soundly.

ANTONIA TRUDGED SLOWLY up the stairs. She'd arrived home the night before, to find Michael gone, leaving no word as to his destination. After sleeping late and partaking of a leisurely breakfast, she'd hoped for some communication, but thus far, none had come. Unhurriedly, she sank into the scented bath awaiting her.

Time was of no concern, so she soaked at length, revelling in the heat whilst her mind mulled over her father's disclosures. She was the veriest shrew. Michael had done much for her, had tried so hard. She remembered his words on their wedding night—that he wasn't sorry, and not for the reasons she supposed. Was he sorry now? Had her actions driven an unalterable wedge between them?

"M'lady?" She emerged from her musings to find Polly standing over her, proffering a sealed envelope. "Tanner brought this; you're to read it immediately."

Antonia snapped upright, spraying droplets, drying her hands on the towel Polly offered. The envelope bore the crest of the Earl of Montewilde, and she hastily tore it open. "The Earl of Montewilde requests the pleasure of his wife's presence at Montewilde Park." Her eyes dwelt on the easy scrawl so at variance with the formal summons. A smile trembled on her lips.

"Tanner said the earl would have you with him this night," said Polly. "It means you'll arrive after dark, but you'll have the coachman, an outrider and Tanner as escorts. He'd like to leave by three, ma'am."

"Is my portmanteau still packed?"

"I can have it ready in a trice."

"Excellent. We'll have no problem being ready on time."

"Tanner brought a note for the butler, too," Polly ventured. "He's closing the town house for the summer. There's ever so much packing to do...."

Antonia smiled. "Why don't you stay here and pack, and come with the other servants? It will be no hardship for me."

"Yes, ma'am," Polly answered with a smile of relief.

At three o'clock, Antonia once again stepped into the coach. Michael had beckoned, and she'd gladly travel the world over if he so desired her presence. The *pleasure* of her presence, he had written. Had he talked with her father? He must have, lest how would he have known she was in London? Had he gone in search of her? She caught her breath. What had her father told him? Surely he wouldn't disclose her innermost secrets? She willed her heart to a normal pace, and forced herself to relax against the squabs. Her father hadn't spoken for Michael; he certainly wouldn't speak for her.

For the first time since their wedding, she had hopes for their marriage. For her and Michael, together. 'Twould be unnerving facing him again. Would he be polite and charming, or stiff and formal? She pressed her hands together, hoping for an open, welcome reception. Or, at least, a courteous one.

Uneasy thoughts absorbed her during the journey, and all the while tension frizzled her nerves. She had no clear notion of the passage of time, but it was dark when the coach finally shuddered to a halt.

"Stand and deliver!" a deep voice proclaimed.

Antonia froze, then righted herself on the seat. Her mouth gaped with awe, and she snapped it shut, cautiously flicking back the curtain to peer outside. The half moon and meagre light of the coach lantern illuminated the dark night.

"Throw the pistol down, man," came a growling, muffled voice. To her right, the dull thud of a heavy weight hit the earth.

"Here now, guv," said the coachman, "we ain't got nothin' you'd want. You'll find slim pickin's 'ere, I guarantee."

"Stubble it!" the muffled voice barked. "You! Get down and open the door. Empty the coach of persons, and mind, no funny play, or you'll be a dead man."

Seconds later, the door was wrenched open, revealing the wide-eyed outrider. Antonia cast him a disbelieving glance, but gave him her hand to be assisted from the coach. Bemused, she took stock of the situation.

There were two men, fully masked in some sort of black material. Cut-away holes served for the eyes and nose. They looked incredibly sinister. One trained a gun on the coachman and Tanner, who sat with their hands in the air. The second, the one giving orders, received the whole of her attention.

"Is that it?" he grunted to the outrider, who nodded silently. "Get away then," he rasped, motioning for him to return to the box. After an apologetic glance at his mistress, the man hastened to do the highwayman's bidding.

The masked man urged his great bay forward, lifting the lantern from its hook. In a fluid motion, he manoeuvred his mount towards Antonia. Holding the lantern aloft, he scrutinized her from head to toe.

"Nothing I'd want, eh?" came his muffled murmur. "My good man, this is a prize to outshine all others, a jewel beyond compare."

Antonia tilted her head at a haughty angle. "Sirrah!" she said in tones befitting a countess, "we've nothing you could want, save the few coins in my reticule, which I'll gladly hand over. I pray you let us be about our business." She opened her reticule, glad for the glove hiding her beautiful wedding ring. How ironic, she thought, that after she'd lied about highwaymen stealing her ring, it should truly happen.

"That won't be necessary," said the man in black. "Your gold holds no interest for me.... You, however, do." He quenched the light, tossing the lantern aside.

A deep, quick breath filled Antonia's lungs. His purring voice, muffled through the cloth, sent a shiver tingling down her spine. Though she could scarce see his eyes, she guessed his intentions. Lifting her skirts, she whirled away.

Before she'd taken two steps, she was captured by a strong arm and scooped into the saddle. With great ease, the highwayman settled her before him.

CHAPTER TWENTY-TWO

ANTONIA STRUGGLED, anger at his audacity overriding fear. His arms were like a vice; her struggles weakened. "Easy now," he purred, "we shouldn't want you to be harmed. And you shan't be if you remain biddable."

She spared a glance towards the ground, finding it a long way off. The beast was huge, bigger than Michael's black. It snorted and tossed its head, and she sensed its power. Ceasing her struggles, she asked through gritted teeth, "What about my men?"

"They'll escape unharmed. We're not in the killing business."

"Comforting words," she snapped.

He chuckled through his mask, wheeling his great mount about. To his partner, he said, "Watch them carefully... and do see I'm not disturbed tonight." The laughter in his voice was unmistakable, and in a fury, Antonia brought her elbow back to connect with his ribs.

He grunted at the impact. "A spitfire, eh? Good, I like spitfires. But, since I can't endure abuse all night..." He produced a length of strong cloth from his coat pocket. Deftly, he bound her wrists before her. In her ear, he whispered, "You force me to be less than chivalrous. Be quiet, or I'll gag you as well."

Antonia had no doubts he would, so clamped her teeth against a stinging retort. Her abductor laughed softly. The huge beast sprang into a run, throwing her against his chest.

He held her and controlled his mount with a skill she had to admire. However, he was but an impudent knave, and she fumed at his high-handed treatment.

She had no idea where he was bound, and refused to ask. His embrace, though tight, was gentle, and she realized she wasn't afraid. Her rage denied any other emotion. Keeping her eyes sharp on their surroundings, she assimilated what she knew of this kidnapper, this highwayman who dared to steal away the Countess of Montewilde. Obviously, he had no care for his hide.

Well educated, from the sound of his speech, she decided. Certainly no peasant ruffian, one of those coarse men who made women shiver by a mere look. Odd, but she didn't feel her life was at stake. There was no telling what lay behind that mask; she'd caught only a glimpse of his eyes. He smelled clean. His cool breath fanning her cheek didn't reek of stale gin or tobacco. An enigma, to be sure, and a dead one when Michael caught up with him.

He manoeuvred the beast off the road and onto a trail leading through a thicket, and she recognized familiar territory. They halted before a small cottage she knew well. They were on Montewilde land, and the cottage belonged to Michael.

They'd played here as children, slaying imaginary dragons which dared come near the door, and intimidating all manner of trolls and other gruesome beings their active imaginations had conjured. Because it was a favourite place with them, the late earl had kept it in good repair, taking no chances of the roof falling in. She stiffened at this sacred ground being sullied by this highwayman.

He dropped the reins and dismounted, then gathered her in a strong embrace. She struggled angrily, and he chuckled. "A pity my mouth isn't free.... Your movements incite a kiss."

She ceased, haughtily straightening away. He ushered her inside the cottage, and bolted the door. A small fire crackled in the grate, shedding meagre illumination in the room. "Will you leave your animal uncared for, sirrah?" she deigned to ask.

"You'd like a chance to escape, eh?" She sensed his smile. "My partner will see to him. I daresay he'll bring your baggage as well, leaving it at the door, of course. I doubt we'll even hear him, being otherwise occupied."

His eyes roved slowly over her. Her breath hissed between her teeth. He moved to the hearth, withdrawing a lantern from the mantel. Lighting it, he held it aloft, allowing her a view of the single room.

It was surprisingly clean, the wooden table scrubbed and flanked by two chairs. The lone set of cupboards was cleaned of the grime she remembered, as was the pot hanging above the fire. A basin and pitcher stood on a small table next to a fluffy, comfortable-looking bed covered by a patchwork quilt. Her eyes flew to those of her captor.

His dark eyes twinkled in a reckless manner. "How do you like our love nest, my beauty?"

"You shan't get away with this!" she hissed. "I am a married woman! I am the Countess of Montewilde. My husband is the Earl of Montewilde—"

"I would suppose him to be, if you're his countess."

She ignored his interjection. "You're on my husband's land, living in a cottage belonging to him. That's crime enough, but he won't countenance you laying a hand to me." Eyes narrowed, she drew herself to her full height. "He'll have your head!" she declared in lowering tones. "He'll see you drawn and quartered! Your cheeky neck will sway from the nearest branch before sunrise!"

Instead of melting with dread, the impudent rogue fell onto a chair and roared with laughter. "You put me in a quaking of this bloodthirsty husband."

"My husband isn't bloodthirsty. He's good, kind, just and honourable. But I swear, he won't take this lightly. He's skilled with both sword and pistol, and handy with his fists as well. If you've any love of your hide, you'll release me now."

Her abductor gave a mocking shudder. "I'm convinced I haven't a prayer against this paragon of virtues. If such a one does exist."

"You don't believe I'm wed?" she queried frostily. "Free me and I'll show you my ring. No doubt you'll steal it," she added scathingly, "though I prize it greatly."

He rose languidly. "You sound as if you love this husband of yours."

"With all my heart," she said softly, so softly he might not have heard had he not been standing directly before her.

His chest swelled with a deep, indrawn breath. A light flickered momentarily in his dark eyes before he bent his head to unbind her wrists. "And does he love you?" came his low, muffled question.

"I rather think it's none of your concern," was her clipped reply. She'd hoped the revelation of her love for her husband would cool the ardour she sensed in the gentleman rogue. Though she wasn't fearful, the veiled threat to her virtue unnerved her. She waited warily to see if her words had made any impact.

"Ah, so you think he doesn't." Her wrists freed, he looked up, lifting a hand to brush a curl from her face. His gloved fingers lingered, resting lightly on her temple. "Were you my wife, I'd love you well. I wonder a man could help but fall in love with a woman of such beauty and spirit. No doubt he's helpless, trapped in a silken web of love and desire. I become more captivated each moment I pass in your presence."

His words, though muffled, caressed her. His long lashes hid his expression. For a moment she dreamed Michael spoke, and she realized how much her heart ached to hear such words of love from him. Thoughts of Michael awaiting her at Montewilde Park returned her to the urgency of the situation. She slapped his hand away. "I'm not your wife."

"Well spoken!" his voice rasped harsh and muffled through the cloth. "But, my sweet, I've every intention of remedying that. I shan't live a daily hell of scorn, and I'll keep you within these four walls until I receive fully of your love!"

Something in his voice arrested her . . . the intent, perhaps, lacing his bold words. Possibly the words themselves. She took a step back, regarding him warily. She hadn't thought . . . could he be mad? No man, save her husband, had the right to say such things. She took another step back, searching the hooded dark eyes.

Dark eyes, shuttered by thick, drooping lashes. Her own eyes narrowed with uncertainty. Clad from head to toe in unrelieved black; the pistol holstered at his side lending him a rakish, dangerous air. . . . But the broad shoulders, lean hips, strong arms— She flew at him, pummelling his chest with her fists. "Beast! Wretch! *Miserable* man! Audacious, impertinent—*I* shall have your head!"

His full-throated laugh filtered through the mask. He captured her arms with the utmost ease, lowering them to her sides before pulling her close against him. "You said you'd as lief marry a highwayman. My darling wife, I would do *anything* to oblige you."

Her struggles ceasing, she gazed into the dark eyes now regarding her openly, love and entreaty shining in their depths. She loosed a hand, lifting it to draw the hood from his head. His hair was mussed; his smile exuded that attractive, dashing charm she so admired.

Tossing the hood aside, she pulled his mouth to hers, savouring the contact. Her lips moved against his in a softly seductive manner which poured forth the wealth of her love, and her other hand crept to his neck. With a shuddering sigh, he captured her close.

Finally, drawing back, she rested in the circle of his arms, gazing at him tenderly. "You're a perfect wretch. Did you order this scene to extract a confession of love?"

His gloves thudded to the floor. He cupped her face between his palms. "Ah, but I didn't know you loved me. All I knew was that I wanted you close...all to myself, all alone. Did I frighten you? It wasn't very gallant of me, but the alternative was worse. Facing each other across miles of dinner table, constantly interrupted by footmen. I couldn't bear resolving our differences in so formal an atmosphere. All the servants and no idea what to expect from you. Do you really love me, or were you trying to bluff the highwayman?"

His expression was hopeful, humble. Her smile was soft, adoring. "I really do. Do you love me, or were those the words of a bluffing highwayman?"

"With all my heart," he murmured. "With all my soul..." His dark eyes smouldered and he expelled a ragged sigh. "I love you more than words can express."

Her eyes misted, and she hugged him tightly. "Why did you never say so? I would have married you immediately. It could have saved us so much pain."

He didn't answer, merely held her before setting her away. His fingers fell to the belt at his waist; he unhooked the clasp and set the pistol on the table. His smile was a trifle wan. "I was afraid. After all that's passed between us, I rather thought you despised me. Or at best, held me at a guarded distance. Whenever I got close, you'd draw away, leaving me to think you wanted nothing of me outside our plot."

He moved to the door, unbolting it. "You let Alex kiss you, and I was consumed with jealousy. You evaded my questions at the inn, jumped away like I was a leper. How could I confess my love when I was sure it would be rejected?" It was a plea for understanding, more than a question. "When we married, I felt the full force of your rejection, and I hated every moment. But I wasn't sorry. I disliked deceiving you, but I'd succeeded in making you my wife, and I didn't care by what means. All that mattered was I loved you, and you were mine."

He shut the door again and bolted it. "Your portmanteau, m'lady," he said, grinning. "Tanner really is the most noiseless man I know. Your father loaned me some wine. 'Tis the one thing I forgot." He opened the case, nodding with satisfaction and approval. "One of his finest, I see."

Antonia giggled. "My father helped you abduct me? What a scamp!"

"He was willing to do anything to promote our happiness. It worked rather well, don't you think?" He held aloft the bottle, his chuckle throaty. "This, my dear, was his weapon."

She laughed outright. "And Tanner? His was perhaps a sausage?"

"Oh, no, his was very real." He slanted her a glance as he opened the wine. "He had to protect you, my love, till he surrendered you into my hands."

She watched him withdraw two cups from the nearly bare cupboard. *My love...* Would her heart ever resume its normal rate? Michael loved her.

"A toast, to us, and to honesty." His cup clinked against hers. "Your father suggested the use of that trait might be conducive to a happier relationship."

She drank with him, then he removed the cup from her unresisting fingers. Scooping her into his arms, he captured her lips in a sweet kiss and moved to the bed. Depositing her gently, he lowered himself beside her.

"Your father couldn't guess your feelings for me, but rather thought you were willing to work things out. Together we schemed our final scheme, for the purpose of placing you in this precise position." His eyes smiled into hers. "We do rather well together, don't you think? You've a knack of falling admirably into our plans."

"My father knows me too well," Antonia replied with a grin of her own. Her father was a complete hand. How she would've loved to watch him manoeuvre Michael as easily as he had her.

"Ah, so he does. He knew about the millpond. Did you tell him all?"

"As much as he needed to know." Her eyes twinkled. "But not that you nearly ravished me."

He stared at her, a myriad of emotions chasing across his face. Memories, she knew, rushed at him with the same force they did her. He groaned, burying his face in the soft curve of her neck. "Oh, Annie, sweet, idiotic, impatient, madcap Annie," he moaned.

He lifted his head, smoothing his palm lovingly over her cheek. One by one, he loosened the pins from her hair. "If only I'd realized you loved me! I would've been kinder, I promise. You were the prettiest girl I knew, and at the time, I rather thought that when you were presented, I'd set myself to be your most assiduous admirer." He gazed into her eyes. "And then the millpond. You were so desirable, your body so soft, so lovely. I was more angry with myself. 'Tis no wonder you hated me."

"Oh, not hate, Michael," she whispered, slipping her fingers through his thick locks. "I never quite managed that, no matter how hard I tried. I didn't mean it when I said so on our wedding night. After the millpond, I locked my feelings away and swore I'd never love again. Which is precisely why I withdrew from you at every turn. But the feelings kept surfacing; they wouldn't rest. I finally acknowledged them."

She sighed. "But we were involved in a Plot, and I couldn't trust that you cared. *I* couldn't bear the thought of *your* rejection. Not again. By the time we married, I had hopes you returned at least a portion of my regard. And then the letter. Oh, Michael, I could scarce bear the ache!"

He hugged her close, one hand caressing her back, the other tangling in the silky mass of her hair. "My poor sweet. What a mishmash! Three years...why didn't you tell me then? It could have saved us so much trouble and pain."

"Michael," she explained, her eyes twinkling, "young ladies don't go about telling young men they love them. To bring a man up to scratch, a lady must needs use a means more subtle. A cramp in the millpond, for instance. He's then supposed to realize, finally, that he's madly in love with her."

"Thank you for the education," he murmured. "You're quicker than I, for it took more than a cramp in the millpond to bring me about. It took Alex stealing you away." He paused, considering. "Maybe it took a dazzling ballgown and a provocative smile. Or seeing you kissed by another...or the feel of your waltzing light as a feather in my arms. Perhaps it took Uncle George to conjure a madcap scheme, or the sight of your beautiful body in a wet chemise." He trailed a finger down her cheek to her neck. "In all likelihood, I probably fell in love at the age of six with my first peek of Rodney's new baby sister. I've been a positive slowtop, Antonia. I promise never to be so again."

"Then you'd best step up the pace, m'lord." Her grin teased. "We've been in this cottage more than an hour, and I'm still fully clothed."

"'Odso!" His eyes danced with laughter. "An oversight I'll rectify with all haste! But first, m'lady, will it sit ill with you to be loved in a highwayman's hut, rather than an earl's mansion?"

"I'm sure being loved in an earl's mansion will be glorious, but for now, I find myself partial to this highwayman's hut."

His chuckle was delightfully husky. "I'm glad. I'm discovering I'm not the most patient of men. But I warn you, my countess, I'm going to love you slowly... very, very slowly."

"Just so long as you love me, I'm sure I shan't mind."

HARLEQUIN'S "BIG WIN" SWEEPSTAKES RULES & REGULATIONS

NO PURCHASE NECESSARY TO ENTER OR RECEIVE A PRIZE

1. Alternate means of entry: Print your name and address on a 3" × 5" piece of plain paper and send to the appropriate address below:

In the U.S.	**In Canada**
Harlequin's "BIG WIN" Sweepstakes	Harlequin's "BIG WIN" Sweepstakes
P.O. Box 1867	P.O. Box 609
3010 Walden Ave.	Fort Erie, Ontario
Buffalo, NY 14269-1867	L2A 5X3

2. To enter the Sweepstakes and join the Reader Service, scratch off the metallic strips on all of your BIG WIN tickets #1-#6. This will reveal the values for each Sweepstakes entry number, the number of free books you will receive and your free bonus gift as part of our Reader Service. If you do not wish to take advantage of our Reader Service but wish to enter the Sweepstakes only, scratch off the metallic strips on your BIG WIN tickets #1-#4. Return your entire sheet of tickets intact. Incomplete and/or inaccurate entries are ineligible for that section or sections of prizes. Torstar Corp. and its affiliates are not responsible for mutilated or unreadable entries or inadvertent printing errors. Mechanically reproduced entries are null and void.
3. Whether you take advantage of this offer or not, on or about April 30, 1992, at the offices of D. L. Blair, Inc., Blair, NE, your Sweepstakes numbers will be compared against the list of winning numbers generated at random by the computer. However, prizes will only be awarded to individuals who have entered the Sweepstakes. In the event that all prizes are not claimed, a random drawing will be held from all qualified entries received from March 30, 1990 to March 31, 1992, to award all unclaimed prizes. All cash prizes (Grand to Sixth) will be mailed to the winners and are payable by check in U.S. funds. Seventh Prize will be shipped to winners via third-class mail. These prizes are in addition to any free, surprise or mystery gifts that might be offered. Versions of this Sweepstakes with different prizes of approximate equal value may appear at retail outlets or in other mailings by Torstar Corp. and its affiliates.
4. Prizes: (1) ★ Grand Prize $1,000,000.00 Annuity; (1)First Prize $25,000.00; (1)Second Prize $10,000.00; (5)Third Prize $5,000.00; (10)Fourth Prize $1,000.00; (100)Fifth Prize $250.00; (2,500)Sixth Prize $10.00; (6,000) ★ ★ Seventh Prize $12.95 ARV.

   ★ This presentation offers a Grand Prize of a $1,000,000.00 annuity. Winner will receive $33,333.33 a year for 30 years without interest totalling $1,000,000.00.

   ★ ★ Seventh Prize: A fully illustrated hardcover book published by Torstar Corp. Approximate Retail Value of the book is $12.95.

   Entrants may cancel the Reader Service at any time without cost or obligation (see details in Center Insert Card).
5. This Sweepstakes is being conducted under the supervision of D. L. Blair, Inc. By entering this Sweepstakes, each entrant accepts and agrees to be bound by these rules and the decisions of the judges, which shall be final and binding. Odds of winning in the random drawing are dependent upon the number of entries received. Taxes, if any, are the sole responsibility of the winners. Prizes are nontransferable. All entries must be received at the address on the detachable Business Reply Card and must be postmarked no later than 12:00 MIDNIGHT on March 31, 1992. The drawing for all unclaimed Sweepstakes prizes will take place on May 30, 1992, at 12:00 NOON, at the offices of D. L. Blair, Inc., Blair, NE.
6. This offer is open to residents of the U.S., the United Kingdom, France, Germany and Canada, 18 years or older, except employees and immediate family members of Torstar Corp., its affiliates, subsidiaries, and all the other agencies, entities and persons connected with the use, marketing or conduct of this Sweepstakes. All Federal, State, Provincial, Municipal and local laws apply. Void wherever prohibited or restricted by law. Any litigation within the Province of Quebec respecting the conduct and awarding of a prize in this publicity contest must be submitted to the Régie des loteries et courses du Québec.
7. Winners will be notified by mail and may be required to execute an affidavit of eligibility and release, which must be returned within 14 days after notification or an alternate winner will be selected. Canadian winners will be required to correctly answer an arithmetical, skill-testing question administered by mail, which must be returned within a limited time. Winners consent to the use of their name, photograph and/or likeness for advertising and publicity in conjunction with this and similar promotions without additional compensation.
8. For a list of our major prize winners, send a stamped, self-addressed ENVELOPE to: WINNERS LIST, P.O. Box 4510, Blair, NE 68009. Winners Lists will be supplied after the May 30, 1992 drawing date.

Offer limited to one per household.